MIRROR-WALKER III
Master of the Mirror

Mitchell Micone

MIRROR-WALKER III
Master of the Mirror

ISBN: 978 1 78695 166 3

Fiction4All
www.fiction4all.com

This Edition
Published 2017

Chapter One
Intrusion

Lieutenant Harold Tecumseh Anderson sat with his back against the wall in the dimly lit room. He rocked on the back legs of the small folding chair and curved his body forward to more intently study the readings on the electronic instruments in front of him. His head lowered even further as he strained to read some of the smaller displays on the equipment which was stacked precariously on the small tray table. He glanced up for just a moment as Major Allen Gretz paced nervously near him in the small walkway.

The major's bald head, with a touch of gray in the fringe, proclaimed that he was approaching his fifties. The rest of his body defied that age and looked much younger. Despite having been at what others called "a desk job" for a number of years, he had not allowed his combat-ready body to soften. His muscular shoulders barely fit between the rough copper screening which covered the plexiglass outer wall of the security area and the smooth gray metal walls of the first row of cabinets. Inside those cabinets were the many memory modules which made up the top secret data vault called "Shangri-la."

The major pressed his back against the metal cabinets and raised himself on tiptoe so he could squeeze past Lieutenant Anderson and his equipment. He grunted out, "Anything?" as he slid past. The major's voice echoed slightly in the aisleway as he squeezed past and repeated that question to each of the dozen other men and women watching similar readouts along the perimeter of the room.

The major hadn't expected anything from the lieutenant. Harold was too new– too inexperienced in the shadowy world of military espionage and counterespionage– to pick up the nuances of potential threats. He was, after all, just a shavetail right out of West Point. What did he know about the world of spies and counter spies? True, he had graduated near the top of his class with a specialty in electronic engineering. That was a plus in his favor, but he was still a "special placements student"– meaning extraordinary political influence had been used to give him his place at The Point.

That appointment worked both for and against Lieutenant Anderson in Major Gretz' mind. The major hated politics and politicians with a passion and had seen too many special-placements soldiers fail miserably. But he had heard from his friends at The Point that this particular student was not a slacker despite his political leverage. In addition, the lieutenant appeared to have an exceptional knack for anything electronic. His intuitive understanding of how almost any electronic circuit worked was what had first caused him to come to the attention of Major Gretz. In the final analysis, it was also what ultimately overcame the major's reservations about putting someone so inexperienced on his team.

For Harold, this operation was a chance to prove himself to the major. Someone was hacking into one of the most secure data depositories in the world and Major Gretz' group had been tasked with the responsibility of finding out who... and how.

The room in which they were sitting was located almost a mile beneath a granite mountain. No person could enter or leave the facility except through a series of elevators and guard stations with very rigid security protocols.

The room itself was a room within a room which sat in the middle of a large, domed cavern that had been carved out of the rock. The heavily-shielded plexiglass walls– which prevented any radio signal from leaving the room– were separated from the cut rock of the cave by a meter-wide walkway all the way around. The floor was raised by a similar amount. To prevent a wire of any sort from being surreptitiously installed from beneath, three totally-independent sets of clear support columns for the floor were raised or lowered hydraulically on a random basis. Likewise, the electrical supply was routinely switched between three separate feeds which were totally replaced on a regular basis. In addition, large fans with blades that extended out nearly twelve feet moved on tracks over the top of the room to sever any wire that should not be present. There were also surveillance cameras mounted on the trolleys which carried the fans.

Nothing was left to chance. Except for "the umbilical," a narrow, clear plexiglass walkway which connected the room to the elevators, the room was totally cut off from the outside world. No signal of any sort could enter or leave the data room except by way of one very heavily-firewalled, monitored, and encrypted data cable that hung from the ceiling of the umbilical. And yet, despite all that, some unauthorized person was accessing the data stored there and offering it for sale on the dark web.

Such access was impossible, and not just because of the extreme isolation of the room. The computer equipment was just as isolated. Any person desiring access to Shangri-la's data had to be on a special list and had to attempt connection from a specific place– or at least a place with a specific, pre-approved IP address. Even if all that computer information was properly spoofed and the rogue computer was incorrectly identified as legitimate by the security software, it would not be enough to access the data. That would only get you in the front door.

In order to connect to the database itself, a properly-authorized human being had to call in on a totally separate, special, secure, telephone and use the proper protocol to request the final access code. There was a random, one-time encryption used for each of those calls, so the line was absolutely secure. When a call was received and electronically verified, a human operator in the data center would verbally re-verify everything before typing the correct daily password into their terminal. Then the database computer, itself, generated a random, ten-digit alphanumeric code on a screen in front of the operator that was good for only forty seconds. Speaking into an old-fashioned ear-trumpet-style mouthpiece that hid her lips from all observers, the operator would read that code to the person on the secure phone so they could type it into the computer on their end as she spoke. Only then would access be granted. Such a connection scheme is absolutely unhackable, and yet, someone, somehow, was getting into the database.

After an intensive review of all procedures and an extremely in-depth investigation of all operators, it was surmised by a group of white-hat hackers and other experts employed by the Pentagon that the most likely vulnerability was some sort of bug or intercept that was picking up the access code from within the computer room itself. How that code was being transmitted from the hyper-secure room or how exactly, that code was being used to attack the database was not yet known, but everyone was absolutely sure that whatever was happening was somehow happening under the mountain in the computer vaults themselves. Thus, Major Gretz and his team were scanning for any indication of an unauthorized device or transmission.

Harold looked up from his meters at the operator

sitting almost in front of him in a small cubicle created by leaving out one section of the memory cabinets. She was facing away from him, but he could just make out the image of her face in the monitor screen which was positioned in front of her. She was beautiful, as would be expected in her position.

Jokes are often made about the fact that high-level people often have beautiful secretaries, but there is a security reason for such beauty. That reason has to do with sex. Sex is the favorite– and most effective– weapon that spies have used throughout history. Men, as a general rule, are very susceptible to seduction. Young, old, handsome, ugly, it is normally just a matter of finding the right woman– or sometimes man– for the job. The old cliché about the beautiful spy is not far from truth, though in reality, the beautiful woman is normally just one more tool that the actual spy has in his or her arsenal.

Women in high-security positions can also be seduced, of course. But a female's response to attempted seduction is different and varies depending upon the woman's beauty. Ugly women will probably know that you just want to use them if you try to seduce them... but history has shown that ugly women are very susceptible to someone who treats them kindly and politely. A pretty, but plain, woman, or a woman who is almost beautiful is the easiest target. She will often fall head over heels for someone who finally shows her romantic attention and tells her that she is, indeed, beautiful. A very famous White House intern falls in this category.

A truly beautiful woman, on the other hand, takes such things for granted. She is used to people treating her with deference. She is used to men trying to put the moves on her. She is used to being told that she is pretty or sexy or beautiful or whatever. That makes her, for all intents and purposes, immune to seduction espionage.

9

That is why, from a security point of view, it is best to have beautiful women in highly-sensitive positions.

From Harold's point of view, it wasn't a bad idea either. He sighed slightly as he watched the reflection of the very comely miss in the monitor across the narrow aisleway from him. He couldn't hear her– or see her lips– as she slowly read the code phrase into her headset.

He smiled at her anyway.

She must have been watching him also, because she pushed the mouthpiece slightly to the side so he could see her mouth curl upward as she smiled back. Then, for just an instant, her face was gone from the dim monitor screen. Her blond hair, white teeth, and red-lipped smile were replaced with dark hair, dark eyes, and a stern– almost frightening– expression on what was obviously a man's face.

Harold didn't know how he knew, but he knew. Images that were not his memories flashed through his mind as he suddenly jumped to his feet and began yelling, "Intrusion! Intrusion! Intrusion! Shut it down! Shut it down! Shut it down!"

Alarms sounded throughout the facility as the small table in front of him tumbled to the floor spilling equipment across the narrow walkway.

"What have you got, Lieutenant?" Major Gretz barked out as he rushed up to him.

Harold took several quick breaths and then, standing rigidly at attention, said in a slightly quaking voice, "I can't tell you, sir."

"Are you saying you just put this entire facility on lockdown and don't know what it was that caused you to do that?" the major asked brusquely.

"No sir," Harold snapped back, his voice becoming more assured. "I'm pretty sure I know exactly what it was, sir... but I can't tell you." He paused and swallowed, "I need to talk to Secret Service Special Agent Mark Nash first... sir."

"I don't know what the hell you think you're doing, Lieutenant," the major snapped back angrily, "but this is a highly-classified, top-secret project and I am not going to have you talking to anyone about anything happening in this room."

Harold looked at his superior officer and said calmly, "Major, you know the story of how I was appointed to West Point, right?"

"Yes," Major Gretz answered. "You got involved in some weird secret shit involving some high-level person and they rewarded you by getting you a Presidential appointment to West Point."

"That high-level person," Harold replied, "was the First Lady of the United States and that weird secret shit is what I think I just now saw happen. I need to talk to the Secret Service agent who was involved in that weird shit with me to find out if this was just them doing something neither you nor I am supposed to know about... Sir."

The major looked at him in silence for a long time and then said softly, "Damn."

After a long pause he asked, "Who is this agent you need to speak with?"

Chapter Two
Friend or Foe?

Special Agent Mark Nash felt his official cellphone vibrate slightly in his pocket. That was followed by a tone and a chirp which indicated a high-priority message. If they were in public, he would still ignore the call unless it went to the emergency code. But since they were within the White House grounds and he wasn't directly guarding the First Lady, he looked around to see who was nearby and then pulled the phone from his pocket.

"Nash," he said firmly.

A soft-spoken operator said, "I have a high-priority call from a Lieutenant Harold T. Anderson which has been placed by Major Allen Gretz and authorized by General William Worthington."

"I'll take the call," Mark responded.

A moment later a voice asked, "Agent Nash?"

"Yes," he replied, "this is Special Agent Mark Nash."

"This is Harold Anderson, I was your escort guard out at Roswell a couple years ago."

"I remember you," Mark answered, glancing around nervously out of habit.

"This is an odd question," Harold said, "but is there any chance that you and your projection friend are doing anything like projecting into the secure data storage vaults at Shangri-la Mountain?"

Mark took a very deep breath as he again checked who was nearby and might overhear him. "No," he replied slowly. "David and Chi are not doing anything like that. Why do you ask?"

"I think someone just projected themselves into the secure server area," Harold said. "I'm not really sure

12

how I know, but I saw this face in the monitor for just a second and I somehow knew it was a mirror-walker coming into the room."

There was a long period of silence as Mark stood totally motionless, thinking. Then he asked firmly, "Who is in the room with you right now?"

"Just Major Gretz," Harold replied.

"Let me speak with him," Mark said evenly.

A few moments later a gruff voice said, "This is Major Gretz."

"What are your security clearances, Major?" Mark asked.

"I'm talking to you from one of the most secure data installations on earth," the major replied almost angrily. "And I have complete access here! What in the hell do you think they are?"

"I would assume at least Top Secret with a Scientific clearance and some fancy words and extra letters going out almost to the end of the alphabet," Mark answered calmly. "But whatever your clearance levels are right now, they are about to get a lot higher. You and Lieutenant Anderson will be receiving classified orders shortly by special messenger. I and a couple of other people whose names you don't yet need to know will meet you at the Pentagon tomorrow. Full details will be included in your orders."

He paused and said, "I don't think I need to tell you that whatever the Lieutenant saw is somewhere beyond anything for which you and your team are currently cleared. No one else is to be apprised of what occurred or what Lieutenant Anderson thinks he saw. Is that understood?"

The major's face showed that he was mentally digesting the implications of what Agent Nash had just told him. He opened his mouth as if he were going to ask something, but instead let out a breath and said firmly,

"Understood."

Chapter Three
It Begins

The orders had been specific that Lieutenant Anderson and Major Gretz were to enter the Pentagon using the Metro entrance on the second level of corridor ten. Someone would meet them at the entrance and escort them to where the meeting would take place. Harold felt a little awkward standing around in the corridor with a major while hundreds of civilians and as many military personnel streamed past them. He was trying to look relaxed while at the same time scanning the crowd with his eyes for any indication of someone walking toward them. Major Gretz, standing alongside him, looked slightly more at ease, but was nervously tapping his fingers against his thigh.

Both startled slightly when a gruff, but feminine voice spoke from alongside them. "Tecumseh?" She said just above a whisper. "... Bradley?"

"Y... Y... yes," Harold answered unsteadily.

"Yes?" Major Gretz answered a little more surely, but with an obvious question in his voice.

The woman stepped around in front of them. There were two stars on the lapels of her uniform. "This will go much quicker if you can answer the following question correctly, Lieutenant," she said quietly. "What color was the van you rode in out at Roswell?"

Harold looked surprised and stuttered out, "Uh... colors don't look right in that bright sun and it was all covered with dust, but I think it was gray. There was another color on it... maybe a reddish brown."

"Close enough," the general said with a smile. "Follow me."

She then turned around and started walking down the corridor. They stopped at the main elevators and waited for one that was going down. When the doors opened two levels down, the general walked across the wide lobby area to another set of elevators. She swiped her badge across a reader and the doors opened. A Marine guard was standing inside.

"Level Sub B2," the general said brusquely.

"Yes, Ma'am," the guard replied and pressed a round fob of some sort that was hanging around his neck against one of the blank circles on the panel next to him. The elevator started down smoothly, but very slowly. Evidently this one, like all Pentagon elevators, was hydraulic rather than cable driven, but for some reason was set to operate much more slowly. That reason, unknown to Lieutenant Anderson and Major Gretz, was to give a longer warning to those on level Sub B2 that someone was arriving.

"One more ride," the general said with a slight laugh when the doors finally opened. Then she added, "Wait here 'til I clear you."

Neither Lieutenant Anderson nor Major Gretz needed further encouragement to wait where they were. Three Marine guards stood just across a small open area. Two of them had their weapons aimed at the open elevator door.

"General Crossford," she said calmly as she held up her ID badge to the third Marine. When the Marines with the raised weapons shifted nervously, she added, "... with two cleared visitors."

The third Marine stepped forward and read the badge. He then pointed what looked like a small flashlight at the general's left eye.

"Verified," he barked out and the other two guards lowered their weapons, but kept them at the ready. She nodded at the elevator on the left and he pressed a button which opened the door.

"Follow me," General Crossford said firmly and the

major and Lieutenant Anderson hustled across the open area to join her in the elevator.

"You might want to hold on to the grips," she said and then pushed the single button on the elevator panel.

Harold yelped as the elevator began rapidly moving sideways. This elevator– if you could call it that– was cable driven and was *VERY* fast. Major Gretz had a look of surprise on his face, but remained silent.

When the door opened this time, Special Agent Mark Nash was standing with two Marine guards. "Verified," he said softly as the door opened, and the guards stepped back against the opposite wall to stand more or less at ease. Their weapons were raised in front of their bodies, however, and their fingers were carefully wrapped around the trigger guards, ready to move into firing position at a moment's notice.

"There's more of them than just David, aren't there?" Harold said softly as he stepped up to face Agent Nash.

"Looks that way," Mark replied, "and you are now part of a team that has to figure out who they are and how to stop them."

"Who are 'them'?" Major Gretz asked in his normal, gruff voice.

"Our worst nightmare," General Crossford, answered, matching his gruffness as she opened a door into what looked like a conference room of some sort. "They are an extremely potent weapon for which we have no defense."

For a moment the major's composure broke. "Damn!" he muttered beneath his breath as he followed Mark and the general into the room.

"David will be observing our meeting," Mark said calmly. He and my brother will be joining us later once we figure out what we have to do."

"Is that a monitor projector?" Major Gretz asked,

pointing at a large device sitting in the middle of the table.

"No," Mark answered, trying to keep a laugh out of his voice. "That is an old-fashioned speakerphone. It is on a one-way connection to my brother Robert, who will tell us if David sees anything out of the ordinary."

"Where is David?" the major asked, looking around the room.

"That," General Crossford answered, "is where this gets interesting." She motioned for the major and Lieutenant Anderson to be seated. Agent Mark Nash sat across from them. The general took the seat at the head of the table.

"Are we alone?" Mark asked the empty seat next to him.

A few moments later, a deep, male voice came over the speakerphone. "David says you are alone. He is coming back now."

"That is my older brother," Mark said. "He is with David, who is standing in his bedroom in Plain City, Iowa, staring into a mirror." He pointed to the empty chair next to him and added with a smile, "He is also sitting here next to me at the table."

"But... but... but..." Major Gretz sputtered.

"He can see and hear everything that is done in this room," Mark said firmly. "He can also understand whatever is said, regardless of what language is spoken." After a pause, Mark added, "And more importantly for us here and now, he can see if there are any other mirror-walkers in the room with us."

The major turned to Lieutenant Anderson and said with very wide eyes, "How did you know? How did you see them?"

"There is only one weakness, as far as we know," General Crossford said slowly. "At the instant a mirror-walker enters a room, they are visible for less than a

18

second in whatever mirror or reflective surface they are using. If you are staring directly into the mirror, you can see their face flash for just an instant."

"I was watching the operator across from me in the reflection on the monitor," Harold said a little sheepishly. "Her face disappeared for an instant and was replaced by a really mean-looking man with dark hair and dark eyes. How I know is much too long a story, but I knew that a mirror-walker had entered the room."

"You now know as much as we do, Major Gretz," the general said with a slight laugh. "And no one except the five of us here in this room and the President know that there is a rogue mirror-walker out there."

The major looked quickly around the table counting silently. He started to ask something, but then he startled and said, "Oh, yes, the invisible one."

"Invisible, but not deaf," Mark said, somewhat heatedly. "Remember that! And also remember that this young man put his body– his physical body– between the First Lady and an assassin at Roswell."

"I'm sorry," the major said quickly. Turning to face the empty chair, he continued, "I meant no disrespect. I'm just a bit overwhelmed by all of this."

"Join the club," General Crossford said. She then turned to the empty chair and said, "David, we need your help to understand exactly what a mirror-walker can and cannot do and if there is any defense against someone like you. We know that you are not willing to be used as a weapon or as a spy, and we have honored that, but as you have heard, the situation has changed. Your country, and perhaps the world, needs you very badly right now. Will you help us?"

A few moments later, Robert's voice came through the speaker. He was laughing slightly. "Two questions and a demand," he said. "Question one: Do you need him there in person or just through the mirror? Question two: Do you need Chi's involvement? And the demand: Anything you discover has to be shared equally with at least the Chinese government."

"Yes, we will need you here– or wherever– in person," Mark answered, addressing the empty chair. "Yes, Chi's help would be useful. We could possibly do it with her just through the mirror, but her physical presence would be much better."

"And yes," General Crossford interjected, "we will share the information with the Chinese government." She laughed slightly, "Especially since we have no way to prevent your friend, Chi, from observing everything that we do anyway."

Looking at the empty chair, Mark quickly added, "Wait a minute, David. Tell my brother that we are also going to need him out here."

The four sat at the table waiting, staring at the speakerphone until Robert said, "David agrees. He is back here now, but is going to go see Chi at Chou's tomb. They have some sort of coded text they can send each other for that." He paused and then continued, "I assume you will clear things with my boss and send us specific instructions. Mark can call me later when he is someplace that cellphones work."

The speakerphone then went silent.

"What is your brother's role in all this?" Major Gretz asked.

"Robert is a detective back in Plain City," Mark answered. "He kept David safe while they rescued the First Lady and later kept Chi and her grandmother safe while they rescued David." He grimaced slightly and said, "Our choices of cleared body guards are pretty slim."

"Is that going to be my role also?" Harold asked.

"Partly," General Crossford answered. "But you have electronics training that might also come in useful.

You will be more of a liaison between David and the teams who will be testing countermeasures against him."

"And me?" Major Gretz asked.

"You will be putting together the best techs and engineers we can find to do that testing," the general replied. "Some of them will have to be read in. Most of them will never know exactly what they are working on or why."

"Understood," the major replied. His face was slightly contorted and his eyes looked like they were scanning something above his head as he already began to think about the process needed to put together a top-secret task force.

Chapter Four
A Roadblock

It is said that most wars are lost because too many generals are fighting the previous war. The disastrous frontal assaults of the American Civil War were done because that was what would have been the winning move in the Napoleonic Wars. The entrenchment of World War I came about partly because such trenches had been the path to victory against the Boers. Between the World Wars, mighty battleships were built to defend the seas against the ships which the old colonial powers had used successfully in "The Great War." But the mighty dreadnaughts were no match for the new weapons of the air when a second World War erupted. And so it goes for generation after generation... Korea... Vietnam... Iraq... and on and on. Again and again, otherwise brilliant military minds are led into abysmal decisions and defeat because they are thinking of how to win the last war, not how to fight the present-day conflict.

Of course, in modern-day America, there is another path to stupidity. Sometimes generals are not thinking of the past war, but rather of the next election. Many in the military were privately– and not-so-privately– saying that with the state of the world, it was time, once again, to have a Commander in Chief with significant military experience. And none were saying that more loudly than the Chairman of the Joint Chiefs of Staff, General Jeremiah Joseph Johansson, known to his friends as "Triple J" and behind his back as "that Son of a J." Triple J knew in his heart that the way to win the next war– which he was sure was coming– was for him to spend eight years as the President of the United States.

Those political ambitions lead General Johansson

to oppose almost any new idea or project proposed by the current President. True, the President had originally appointed him as Chairman of the Joint Chiefs and had the power to remove him from that post, but with the connections Triple J had built up over the years, that would be political suicide. So President Travis did what any man who had honed his skills in the business world would do in the face of such opposition. He just went around General Triple J and did whatever he wanted to do anyway.

Unfortunately, the current project was going to be expensive... very expensive... extremely expensive. To fund such a process without having to explain everything to several congressional committees and subcommittees, the Chairman of the Joint Chiefs of Staff would have to sign off on activating certain Presidential emergency powers. And General Jeremiah Joseph Johansson refused to do so unless "I am personally convinced that all this hocus pocus is not just another of Douglas Travis' famous tap dances through a stage full of smoke and mirrors."

So once again Mark Nash, General Crossford, Lieutenant Anderson, and Major Gretz were gathered in the secret Pentagon conference room. With them this time were Robert Nash and David Malone. The empty chair between them was reserved for Chi. Last to arrive was General Johansson.

"I'm surprised Douglas isn't here himself to try to sell me this load of bull," he said almost angrily as he entered the room and quickly took the seat reserved for him at one end of the table.

It was Mark who answered him from the other end of the table. "President Travis does not need to, as you say, sell this," he began softly. "That's because it is all true. Mirror-walkers exist and are possibly one of the greatest dangers this country has faced in years."

The general just crossed his arms in front of himself on the table and laughed quietly. "We'll see," he said. "We'll see."

"Let me introduce you to the members of our team," General Crossford said quickly.

"I know most of you," General Johansson spit out. He pointed at Mark Nash and began speaking. "Mark Nash, Secret Service favorite of the First Lady; Major Gretz, Army Counterespionage, responsible for super-secret, off-the-books technical projects; Lieutenant Anderson, recent West Point graduate with political connections to Douglas Travis himself; Robert Nash, a detective from Iowa who is here because he is Mark Nash's brother; and, of course, you, Deanna, General in charge of all sorts of mysterious projects for Douglas Travis."

"You left out two people," David said forcefully. "I am David Malone, Mirror Walker from Iowa; and this," pointing to the empty chair, "is Kong Jing, a Mirror Walker from Penglai, Shandong, China."

Triple J began slow clapping while laughing slowing in time to his claps. "Well played! Well played!" he said, continuing his slow laugh. "Douglas has pulled out all the stops for this one– invisible threat... Chinese involvement... all-American boy from Iowa playing mysterious hero. Who could possibly say no to such a combination?"

"Give me a minute," David said, "and I will show you what we are dealing with." He then picked up a small, framed mirror that had been lying flat on the table in front of himself.

"Your secretary's name is Gloria Thomas, correct?" David asked turning the mirror so that the general could see the picture of a very pretty, redheaded woman that was taped in the corner of the mirror.

"Yeah, that's Gloria," the general replied.

24

"Please be quiet," David said. "This is hard enough to do with clothes on, let alone with so many people watching me."

In response, the general just chuckled loudly and shook his head slowly from side to side.

It was hard to concentrate under such circumstances, but after a moment, David felt the familiar pull and suddenly he was through the mirror and standing behind a redheaded secretary. He looked over her shoulder to read the screen on her computer. She was apparently putting the finishing touches on a speech the general was scheduled to give at an event that evening. David read what he could on the screen and then quickly looked around the outer office. Not finding anything useful or important, he pushed his way through the door into the general's private area. He wasn't sure what he was looking for. There was nothing on the desk for what he needed. There was nothing on the walls, either. There might be something in the closets, but that was beyond him. Although he could easily push through the closet doors, he couldn't open them and it would be pitch dark inside. Finally he saw what he was looking for. Sitting on top of the debris in the waste basket under the general's desk were three– no four– no six– crumpled candy bar wrappers.

"Return," he thought softly and suddenly he was back in the conference room beneath the Pentagon.

David took several deep breaths before smiling over at the general and saying, "You must have been nervous about the meeting you have scheduled for tonight, General Johansson, or perhaps I should call it your first, preliminary, campaign rally."

He smiled at the general's slightly startled look and continued, "I was just in your office. Your secretary is working on that "maybe-I'm-running" speech you are supposed to deliver tonight. She is trying to re-write

25

your joke about the truck driver and the toll booth attendant to make it specific to New Hampshire. In your private office, I can see from your wastebasket that you recently depleted your cache of Butterfingers. You ate at least a half dozen of them this morning before coming over here."

"Good guess," General Johansson said as his face hardened. "But it's no secret I'm toying with running for President. And everyone knows I have a weakness for Butterfingers... not to mention the fact that I have used that toll booth joke in almost every speech I have given in the last few months."

Looking around the table he snarled out, "I really expected more than this from Douglas Travis." He then pressed his hands against the table and said, "If that's all you've got, I'm leaving."

David took a quick breath and looked into the mirror. A moment later he was back in the general's office. As soon as the room became visible around him, he said loudly to himself, "Red leather chair, red leather chair, red leather chair."

There was only one red leather chair in the Pentagon conference room. It was the chair in which sat General Jeremiah, Triple J, Johansson and David was about to overlap him.

The general had almost started to rise out of the chair when he yelled out, "What the Hell!!"

His body convulsed slightly and he dropped back into his chair, looking around the room with a very dazed and confused expression on his face.

Across from him David was now breathing heavily and struggling to speak. Finally he pulled himself together and said in a raspy voice, "Here's something I couldn't have guessed. You mistrust the President so much that you have secretly had an override code established that can prevent him from firing our nuclear

26

missiles."

The general just stared back at him.

"That override code," David said slowly, "is zero, zero, zero, one, one, one, two, two, two, three, four, five."

"Tha... tha.. that's impossible," General Johansson sputtered. "Only three people in the world know that code."

"I now also know your mistress' cell phone number," David said firmly. "Would you like me to say that out loud?"

"Holy shit!" Robert said loudly. Turning to Mark he said with wide eyes, "I didn't know he could do *THAT!*"

"I did," said Lieutenant Anderson with a big smile. "He did that accidentally to me out at Roswell. But I didn't know he could do it intentionally."

"Neither did I," David said with a shudder. "And it's even harder on me when I *TRY* to do it."

"Oh, my God!" General Johansson said looking around the room. "Oh, my God!" He repeated and then stared at David saying, "You're real! This is all real!"

"Welcome to my world," Robert said with a laugh. Then pointing to the empty chair, he continued, "Oh... and say hello to Kong Jing. Most of us call her Chi."

"How many of these... mirror-walkers... are there?" the general said slowly.

"Chou thought he was the last," David said very deliberately, "then he met me. I thought I was alone, then I met Chi. And now we know that there is at least one rogue mirror-walker out there stealing secrets and selling them on the dark web." He shook his head and continued slowly, "We really have no way of knowing how many mirror-walkers there actually are."

"And more importantly," General Crossford said firmly, "we know of no defense against them. One of them got into the main data vault control area at Shangri-la Mountain and stole the access codes."

"He probably got the name and image of one of the operators," Mark said. "That's all it takes. And once he had been in the room, he could return at any time even if that operator weren't there."

General Johansson looked around the room. His eyes were wide. "One of them could be walking through the halls of the Pentagon right now," he said slowly.

"Or inside one of our submarines or carriers," General Crossford added. "Or even in the Oval Office."

"What do you need?" General Johansson said flatly.

"Your signature on this Presidential Order," General Crossford replied, sliding a piece of paper across the table. "And someplace *very* secure that hopefully our opposition mirror-walkers have never heard of."

Chapter Five
Copper Harbor

"You want us to go where?!" Robert Nash exclaimed as General Johansson explained the plan which he and Major Gretz had devised.

"It's an old mining port in northern Michigan," the general responded somewhat testily.

"I know where it is," Robert yelled back. "I've been there... in the summertime! There is this great big thermometer-like thing at the edge of town which records the snowfall for the previous winter. The record is somewhere over thirty feet. Last year they got twenty-four feet. And that shit don't melt 'til spring."

"Actually," General Johansson replied calmly. "The snow thermometer is in Calumet, about thirty miles west of Copper Harbor. And we will be in Delaware, which is about half-way in between."

He smiled across the table at Robert and added, "And the three *WINTERS* that I was up there, we had just under thirty feet of snow each year."

"You'll have to excuse my big brother," Mark said with a chuckle. "He has always hated winter and the idea of being totally snowed-in underground for a couple of months of below zero weather is not his idea of heaven."

"You got that right!" Robert huffed.

"But I assume there is a reason for choosing Copper Harbor, Michigan... or was it Delaware?" Mark continued.

"There are several reasons," General Johansson said, looking around the table. "The most important is that the Delaware Copper Mine is willing to lease their entire facility to us for up to six months. The Delaware mine has been closed for decades as an actual mine, but has been kept up as a tourist attraction. They have already closed for the winter, so it is ours from November through April. The place is huge. We can set up housing and everything else underground. And there is a large parking lot that we can keep clear of snow for helicopter take off and landings for most of the winter... at least enough of it."

"Won't that draw attention from the locals?" asked General Crossford.

"A lot of the area residents leave for the winter," General Johansson answered. "And those who stay are mostly mind-your-own-business types of people. Besides, it wouldn't be the first time that the government has leased the mine for the winter."

He smiled at the look of shock on everyone's faces. "Ever hear of Project Sanguine?" he asked, his smile getting even broader.

"E. L. F. submarine communications," David said slowly.

Now it was General Johansson's turn to be surprised.

David shrugged and said, "I'm a war history geek." He then paused a moment and said, "Republic, Michigan... is just across Keweenaw Bay from Copper Harbor."

"OK" Robert said, sounding very flustered. "Would somebody please tell me what all this has to do with trying to find a way to stop this rogue mirror-walker?"

"Back in the sixties... or maybe the seventies..." David began, "the Navy came up with this way of communicating with submarines even when they were down a thousand feet or more at full patrol depth. The transmitters required millions of watts, the land-based antennas had to be miles and miles long, and the subs had to trail a long antenna behind them, but it worked. It took a couple of minutes to send even a single letter, but

30

you could tell a sub hundreds of feet under the water to surface for further communication.

"They found that if you located two of the transmitters just the right distance apart in just the right type of rock, you could make it work without having to dig up most of Montana to lay out an antenna array. Republic, Michigan, and Clam Lake, Wisconsin, were perfect because they were the right distance apart, were isolated, and had the right rock substrata."

"They do it differently now," added the general, "so the whole system's been shut down for quite a while. But every so often, the government tests out some new ideas. And they test them at..." He spread his hands slightly as if asking for input.

"The Delaware Mine," Lieutenant Anderson said firmly.

"So everyone thinks this is just another test of submarine communications," Mark said. "What about security?"

"The snow and cold and isolation are our greatest security," the general answered, "at least against normal humans."

"I'm human!" David said, almost angrily, folding his arms across his chest.

"Sorry," the general quickly replied, "that was a poor choice of words on my part. I should have said against humans with normal abilities."

"What about security against our rogue mirror-walker?" General Crossford asked.

"That requires a calculated risk," the general said slowly. He then turned to the one empty chair at the table and said, "Chi, I think that you and David need to talk about this, but we need you both physically present. One of you has to keep watch for the rogue mirror-walker while the other participates in the tests. I have spoken with my counterparts in the Chinese government and they said that it must be your decision."

He laughed slightly and said, "I was somewhat surprised that they would say that. Their people usually just do what they're told, but then they said that I would understand if I ever met Kong Ling. I understand that's your mother."

"Grandmother, actually," David interrupted, "but it's a long story."

He turned to the empty chair and said, "Chi, I will meet you at Chou's tomb in one hour."

Turning back to the general, he said, "I would prefer to return to my hotel room. I can use the mirror in the bathroom."

"I understand," the general began, "that you normally prefer a black mirror created by painting automotive glass. There is a mirror room just down the hall equipped to your specifications. It is private with a curtained-off area for Detective Nash to sit with you while you are in the mirror."

He turned once again to the empty chair and said, "Similar rooms will be provided at the mine if you decide to come."

"Chi prefers polished brass or bronze," David said as he stood up.

Smiling at the empty chair he said, "We can meet in fifteen minutes."

"The guard will direct you to the mirror room," the general said as David walked toward the door. He then pointed at Robert and indicated that he should follow David.

After both had left the conference room, the general gave a deep sigh and said, "I have never been more concerned for my country."

"Or for the world," General Crossford added.

It was over an hour later when David returned. "Chi agrees," he said as he returned to his seat at the table. "But there are some conditions."

"I assumed there would be," General Johansson replied.

"Most importantly," David began, "Kong Ling must accompany her."

"No problem," the general immediately responded.

"Secondly," David continued, "she wants a Chinese security detail with them and wants to travel as much as possible by Chinese military-controlled aircraft."

The general took a deep breath. "May I ask why?" he said slowly.

It was Mark who spoke up. "Do you remember seeing something in the news about a terrorist attack at the Des Moines airport a couple years ago? A bunch of people got shot up, but there were no deaths."

The general nodded.

"There were, however," Mark continued, "two passengers who mysteriously disappeared during the shooting... and were never found."

The general nodded again.

"That was Chi and Momma Ling," Robert said emphatically. "The whole attack was an assassination attempt. If it weren't for the undercover FBI agent that Mark arranged for, we might not have made it out alive."

He bobbed his head up and down as a way of emphasizing his words as he said, "I don't think Kong Ling wants to risk walking into something like that again."

"OK," the general replied. "What else?"

David smiled and said, "I think this is Mamma Ling's idea also, but she wants a small group of Chinese technical people to observe the tests so they can report

33

directly concerning any countermeasures we might develop."

The general laughed slightly. "I am beginning to understand what they said about Kong Ling," he said. "I look forward to meeting her. Yes, she can arrange her own travel plans into the United States. And, yes, they may bring a group of scientists or techs. We are somewhat limited for facilities, so her total entourage needs to be less than fifteen... including Chi and Kong Ling. I will get in touch with my Chinese counterparts to begin getting things set up."

"Chi came back with me," David said. "She has probably gone back to tell Momma Ling what you just said and things are in process on their end."

"In that case," the general replied, "we can adjourn this meeting. Advance teams are already setting things up in the mine. Four military convoys full of needed equipment will leave supply bases starting tomorrow."

He smiled broadly and then said, "None of them are going to Michigan, however– neither are you. The four convoys are headed for Air Force or National Guard bases throughout the east coast. The equipment will make at least one additional stop before being brought by helicopter to the mine."

"And us?" Mark asked.

"You are going to Madison, Wisconsin, – but not directly. Over the next four days, each of you will travel separately by air or in civilian vehicles... except David. Robert you are to be with him at all times. When you get to the Madison airport, someone from the Wisconsin National Guard will escort you over to the military side of the airport and you will be helicoptered to Indianapolis. After a short stopover, you will be taken to the Delaware Mine from there. We should be ready to start operations next Monday."

Chapter Six
Into the Mine

The general's expectation of starting operations on Monday proved to be a bit optimistic. Huge Chinook helicopters had landed and taken off in the parking lot of the Delaware Mine every few minutes throughout the day on Saturday, Sunday, and Monday, but all of the equipment and personnel were not yet in place.

Interspersed on Monday afternoon were several smaller Black Hawks flown out of Indianapolis by the Indiana National Guard. The pilots of the hawks were told that they were just part of an evacuation drill, but the fact that they were only carrying a couple of people in each bird and were shadowed along their entire route by Army Apaches made them understand that there was something more important and perhaps darker about their passengers. The fact that they had been specifically ordered to not speak with the passengers reinforced that understanding.

As David and Robert stepped down onto the parking lot, the crew chief leaned in close to Robert and said, "I don't know what you secret squirrels are up to, but it must be damned important. Good luck."

Robert merely nodded to him and walked with David across the parking lot to where his brother Mark was standing. "We should probably go inside," Mark said, "but I think David will want to watch this next arrival."

He pointed up at four bright orange US Coastguard helicopters approaching from the north. The two larger copters landed while the smaller ones hovered a short distance away. "Kong Ling insisted on coming in through Montreal," Mark explained as Chi, Kong Ling, and a dozen technicians and security people stepped out onto the asphalt. "The Canadians wouldn't allow the Apache escorts, but that worked out for the best. It was probably more important to have air-sea rescue immediately available as they came across the lakes anyway. Besides, Chi's security people felt more comfortable with Coast Guard birds than Army."

David smiled at Chi as she and Mamma Ling walked up to them. She returned his smile as she pulled her coat more tightly about her small body.

"Let's get inside," Mark said and nodded his head toward the entrance.

General Johansson was waiting for them in the lobby. "The last of the equipment won't be here until tomorrow," he said as the small group gathered around him. So all we are going to do this afternoon is give you a tour of the mine, including the lower sections where they don't normally allow the public."

After walking through several large caverns with green, yellow, and red streaks showing in the rock, they took a side path that was labeled "Maintenance Personnel Only." The path circled downward until they came to a closed door with armed guards standing on each side of it. The general pointed at the door and said, "This entrance goes through a mantrap room like they use in prisons. You can't open the exit door on the other end until the entrance door on this end is closed and locked."

On the other side of the guarded door was a long hallway with a concrete floor. Once everyone was inside the long room, the steel door closed with a loud, echoing clang. The general laughed and said, "The sound of that door slamming shut leaves no doubt that you are locked in down here."

He laughed again and pointed up to one of the cameras above the exit door. "And if the guards on the other side of that wall don't buzz you in," he said loudly, "you could be in here for a very long time."

It wasn't clear if the general had said that for their information or to prod the guard on duty, but the door immediately buzzed loudly and the general pushed it open and gestured for everyone to enter.

"We pay the owners of the mine to keep these lowest levels pumped out," he explained as he guided the group further down into the mine. "They aren't part of the public tours, so we've never had to tear out the old test areas from the 1960s. It's a good working agreement for both sides."

After winding through strangely-shaped hallways, he opened a door and said with a flourish, "The housing quarters have been totally re-furbished. There is cable TV down here but no cell service except for special phones which go through the security system. And you have internet access only in the security room where everything in or out can be monitored."

"That means no late-night porn," Robert said with a laugh, "and no naughty texts to the loved ones back home."

"We will try to respect your privacy," the general bristled, "but considering the implications of what we are dealing with we can only go so far."

"You will get used to Robert," Mark said. "He is a bit uncouth in many ways, but he has a real knack for expressing the situation in its most simple terms."

"In other words," the general said, turning to face Mark, "don't ignore the court jester."

"Something like that," David said. "Plus he is used to thinking like a criminal."

"So, Detective Jester," General Johansson said, turning to face Robert, "what do you say about the security here?"

Answering almost immediately, Robert said, "Your greatest vulnerability is faces and names. Nobody important goes back outside until we are all ready to leave. Anyone who has to go in and out only comes in as far as the first security barrier and they never see anyone on this side of the mantrap room. If our bogeyman gets in it will be through something shiny, so put a big-ass mirror just inside the security wall with concealed, high-speed cameras trained on it twenty-four seven. Put at least one more in the first room on the inside of the mantrap. You can use some sort of computer magic to review the tapes to see if anything came through. It won't give a real-time alarm, but we will know if we have been breached."

"Damn!" the general said loudly. "You nailed almost everything we have set up even though I haven't briefed any of you on it yet."

"Don't ignore the Jester," Mark said with a smile.

"Damn straight," General Johansson said as he looked at Robert through new eyes. "And we never thought about using a high-speed camera to monitor a mirror in the safety room."

"Maybe one of those wall-mounted mirrors that looks like it's been put up by the safety people for forklift operators to see around a corner," Robert replied.

The general turned to one of his aides who immediately replied, "We will have it up and running in both entrances before morning."

"Obviously," the general said, "I am too high profile to stay down here. Too many people know my face and my name and if I am gone from DC for too long, they may send their mirror-walker looking for me. And I need Major Gretz to remain with me to coordinate any support for you and to implement anything you find in the way of security and protection for other facilities. General Crossford will remain here in command of operations. All of the military security people and technicians down here are supposedly on a super-secret mission in the Mideast so they won't be missed while they are here. Hopefully, this all can stay under the radar– or whatever it is– until we have something figured out."

Chi said something in Chinese and Kong Ling said, "There is a thirteen-hour time difference from our home. Chi is very tired. It may take a few days to adapt to night being day and day being night."

"In that case," General Johansson said, "I will leave you in the capable hands of General Crossford and the team. First tests are scheduled for oh nine hundred tomorrow." He and his aides then left.

"I will show you to your rooms," General Crossford said, pointing down a small hallway. As she spoke one of the Chinese security people translated for Chi.

"David and Chi, there are mirror rooms just down the hall from your quarters. David, your mirror is black. Chi, yours is polished brass." She waited for the interpreter to translate and then added, "I hope the size and shape are adequate." After another pause for the interpreter she said, "There is a curtained area in each mirror room so your guards can be present."

"Sounds good," said Robert.

David looked over at Chi and she held up her hands with all fingers up. She then lowered one hand but continued to hold the other up. David nodded his head to indicate he understood. He would meet her at Chou's tomb in fifteen minutes.

***

Chi was standing before her grandfather's tomb crying when David came through the mirror.

"What's wrong?" he asked, putting his hand on her shoulder.

She looked up at him and sobbed out, "Everything!"

He waited while she looked down at the floor and trembled slightly as if holding back more sobs. Finally she spoke. "My mother died in the mirror. My grandfather tracked down the mirror-walker who killed her and struck him down with his bare hands."

Looking up at David she said, "I am afraid for you." She moved her hands so that she was looking at her palms and said, "There are no weapons in the mirror, only your bare hands."

"He won't have any weapons either," David said. "And there will be two of us."

"But you have never been trained in the art of fighting," she said loudly, then her voice began cracking into heavy sobs as she said, "You could die in the mirror."

"As could you," he answered softly, "but we are the only ones who can find this spy, whoever he is, and stop him from harming your country and mine. Or worse, perhaps forcing the start of a war somewhere in the world."

Taking Chi's shoulders in his hands, he turned her so they were looking into each other eyes. "Perhaps the tests they are doing here," he continued, "will find a way for the people in the flesh world to defend themselves against mirror-walkers. Then it won't be necessary for us to track down the rogue. They will be able to do it on their own."

She looked up at him and gave a very weak smile. "You sound like my grandfather," she said. "He always knew the right words to comfort me."

"I think the right words for now," David replied, "are that you– and I– need some sleep because tomorrow will be a very hard and busy day."

Chi leaned forward and kissed him on the cheek.

She then shimmered and disappeared.

David sighed and said, "Mirror room."

A moment later, he was standing in front of the black mirror. Robert's voice from the other side of the curtain asked, "You back?"

"I'm back," David answered as he pulled on his robe. "How did you know?"

"I can tell by your breathing," Robert answered. "You give a deep sigh as you come back out of the mirror."

David pulled his robe more tightly around his body and stepped around the small curtain. "It's bigger than my van," he said, looking around the room.

"Yeah," Robert answered, "but your van had windows."

Chapter Seven
Chasing a Will-o'-the-wisp

"Each day will start here," General Crossford said firmly. There were seven people seated around the oval table in the small conference room. The general sat at one end, Mark, David, and Robert sat to her left. Lt. Harold Anderson, Chi, and Kong Ling sat to her right. Two armed Marine guards stood behind David. Two armed Chinese guards stood behind Chi. They were now wearing People's Liberation Army uniforms. Their insignias identified them as part of the Special Operations Forces.

"There is one thing I want to make absolutely clear from the very start," the general began. "Nothing is unimportant. We are chasing a will-o'-the wisp who can slip in and out of anywhere, anytime. If something doesn't seem right, say something. If you get an odd feeling in the middle of the night, use your intercom to tell the night guards. If you see a flash of light out of the corner of your eye or a shadow that seems to move, tell security. We won't act on everything, but if several people see shadows move or hear odd noises, there will be a response. Do you all understand that?"

Everyone nodded their heads, including Chi after Kong Ling translated for her.

"David and Kong Jing," she continued, now pausing to make sure that Kong Ling had time to translate, "some of what we are going to do might be dangerous. It would be better if your protector was able to watch you directly while you are in the mirror."

She paused and said, "I know that you need the privacy for concentration, but in this case, it would be better if someone were watching you."

"General Crossford," David said softly, "it's more

than concentration. It's much easier to enter the mirror if you are totally exposed to the mirror... and I think a larger mirror bubble is formed when there is better exposure."

"I think the mirrors are large enough for you to see your whole body," she replied.

Robert laughed, "That's not exactly what he means, ma'am. What he means is that it works better if he's naked."

"Oh," the general responded. Her facial expression and body language indicated that she was caught by surprise and was somewhat flustered.

"Robert watched over me while we were working out of my van," David said. "He's seen me naked and I guess I've gotten used to him being in the same room while I go into the mirror."

"Kong Jing says," Kong Ling added, "that I raised her and have seen her naked many times before. It will not be a problem for her." She paused and then said, "And there is no problem with you calling her Chi as the others do."

General Crossford nodded and then asked, "When you are in the mirror...?"

"We're naked," David replied with a slight laugh. "As far as we know it is not possible to take anything into the mirror with us. No clothes, no weapons, no nothing. You can't take anything into the mirror. Not even Chou could do that and he was a Master of the Mirror."

"Then how will you be able to deal with the rogue mirror-walker?" she asked. Her concern was obvious on her face.

"Hopefully we will be able to figure out a way to identify him so that someone can capture him in the flesh world," David answered. "If not, it might boil down to a fight between us in the mirror."

The general looked like she wanted to ask a question, but wasn't sure how to phrase it. Sensing what the question probably was, he continued, "Two mirror-walkers can touch each other. It is almost the same as in the flesh world except there is very little sense of warmth. It is like holding hands with a statue."

As Kong Ling translated, Chi smiled and looked down, obviously embarrassed.

"So there is some substance to your mirror body?" the general asked.

"Yes," David answered, "but I don't know exactly how we interact with the flesh world when we are in the mirror. I can push through most walls, but a thicker or stronger wall requires more effort. And Chi accidentally pushed through the outer wall of a jet in flight and was sucked out by the airstream."

Kong Ling's eyes widened as she heard that, but the rest of her face remained impassive. She glanced over at her granddaughter for a second. Chi had once mentioned that something had happened, but hadn't given details.

The general paused as if thinking and then said, "Our plan for this morning is to run some tests involving David. Chi can observe and tell us if it appears that David is in trouble. Robert and Kong Ling will also watch to see if there are any signs of trouble from your real... physical... flesh... bodies."

David and Chi nodded. Kong Ling had translated the general's words, including her fumbling with a term for their flesh bodies, and Chi laughed lightly into her hands.

"Then this afternoon," the general continued, "I want both of you to roam all over this facility from top to bottom. Learn the layout. See what walls you can— what did you call it? – push through easily and what gives you trouble."

She chuckled slightly, "I also want you to go out

past the front mantrap room and come back in, if you are able to do that. There are several different types of alarm sensors out there. Let's see if any of them are any good against a mirror-walker."

David and Chi now smiled at each other. This would be an opportunity to talk as they wandered around the test facility and the mine.

Lieutenant Anderson now spoke up. "Our first test," he said, "is pretty simple. We are going to see how dim it can get before a mirror-walker can't walk."

David thought about the times when he had pushed through large solid objects or, in one case, an airline cargo container. There had been a slight feeling of disorientation after a while, but he had been able to push through.

"Normally," Harold continued, "we would run a test like this by just turning off the lights, but none of us knows what will actually happen... especially down here. We are deep underground and it will get absolutely dark. There is no ambient light down here so dark really means dark. For all we know, switching everything to pitch blackness could kill a mirror-walker, and we don't know what happens to their body if that happens."

"They die," Kong Ling said flatly. "My daughter died in the mirror. Her body lived just long enough to give birth to Kong Jing."

Chi's eyes filled with water and a tear slipped down her cheek as she listened to her grandmother translate what she had just said.

"Sorry," Lieutenant Anderson said. "I really didn't know."

"There is also a place of fire that can kill a mirror-walker," David said slowly. "When you go through the mirror, it creates a bubble of mirror reality. You can recreate that bubble in a new place if there are enough mirrors or reflective surfaces. But it is still a bubble.

"If you go outside that bubble," he continued, "you are in the realm of chaos. If you are unfortunate enough to go there, the Dogs of Chaos and the Fire Warriors will force you into the pit of fire. That will definitely kill a mirror-walker."

"How did you learn of the... place of fire?" Harold asked.

"Been there... done that," David replied.

"So it is possible to escape the place of fire?" General Crossford asked.

"Only if you have a strong connection to another mirror-walker *AND* that other mirror-walker happens to be asleep when you call for help," David said firmly. "It's not something you can rely on... and I don't know if it would work a second time."

"I've seen that place," Robert said. "Scary stuff. I wouldn't want to go there."

"How did *YOU* see it?" the surprised general asked loudly.

"When he comes back out of the mirror," Robert answered calmly, "for just an instant, you can see where he's been in the mirror. For some reason it's a lot longer if he's with those nasty dogs and weird warriors."

"It sounds like," the general said thoughtfully, "in the instant that the mirror-walker goes into or out of the mirror the two worlds are linked in some visible way."

Harold nodded his head and said, "I think that's part of what we hope to find out in our tests."

"Then let's adjourn to the test room," the general said, standing up.

Everyone followed her lead and stood to leave the room. She and Lieutenant Anderson led the others a little way down the hallway from the conference room to a large room that was split in two by a wall with a large glass window. The larger side was bare except for a single desk in the middle of the room. The smaller side had three desks and a long counter under the window which was stacked with equipment.

"I will be sitting over there," Harold said, pointing to the single desk. "Mark will be sitting in here," he continued, pointing to one of the three desks. "We want both of you go through the mirror directly to him, since you know his face so well. After that, mirror Chi will stay on this side of the glass. Mirror David will join me on the other side for the tests. Everybody got that?"

Everyone nodded or said, "Yes," and then David and Chi, accompanied by their guards, returned to their mirror rooms. Robert sat in the room with David; Kong Ling sat with Chi; the armed guards stood in the hallway outside the doors.

A few minutes later, the intercom on Mark's desk squawked and Robert's voice said, "He's in the mirror."

Shortly thereafter, Kong Ling's voice said, "Kong Jing is now with you."

"OK," Harold said. "David will follow me into the other room and then we will start dimming the lights. Once it gets almost dark, the window will seal off. We will then go to total darkness."

The Lieutenant walked into the bare room and took a seat at the desk. As he sat down, he picked up a set of headphones from the desk and adjusted them to fit properly on his head. "Lights to seventy-five percent," he said firmly.

It got dimmer, but it would have been possible to easily read something with moderate-sized print.

He waited about five minutes and said, "Lights to fifty percent."

Again it got dimmer. Now it would be difficult, but still possible to read.

After another five minutes, he said, "Lights to twenty-five percent"

Now reading would be very difficult, but it was still

possible to see almost clearly.

"Fifteen percent," he said after the five minute wait.

"Ten percent."

"Five percent."

Now everything was more or less a shadow. This time Harold waited a full ten minutes before saying, "Three percent."

The glow of the dials on the equipment was now very visible through the window.

"Seal the window," he ordered.

There was no sound, but the window turned totally black. Evidently it was electronically controlled.

"Let me know at twenty minutes," he said into his headset. Then he asked, "Robert, does everything look normal on your end?"

"Yes" Robert replied.

"OK," the lieutenant said. He then waited silently in the almost darkness until someone from the control room side said, "Twenty minutes."

Again he said, "OK," and added, "Lights to one percent."

He held his hand up in front of his face. For all intents and purposes, the room was dark, but he could still vaguely make out his hand if he held it right in front of his face. "Let's wait a full thirty before going for full dark," he said into his headset. Then he asked, "Robert, everything still OK with David?"

"OK" Robert answered back.

David, meanwhile was walking in small circles around the lieutenant's desk. He was somewhat surprised that he could still see rather well in the almost darkness. Then a voice said, "Thirty minutes," and Harold ordered, "Total darkness."

David could not remember ever being somewhere that was absolutely dark. After just a moment, he became totally disoriented. He wasn't sure if he was facing Harold or one of the outer walls. He reached out his hand, but could feel nothing to tell him where he was in the room. After what seemed like about three minutes, but could have been much longer– or shorter, he started to feel very weak. He thought about pulling out of the mirror, but then decided to stay and complete the test. Shortly after that he collapsed.

He didn't realize that he was falling, but he knew when he crashed into the floor. One of his hands pushed slightly into the concrete and rock. Then it felt like he was spinning– as if he had been sucked up into a giant tornado. He was being pulled apart as if he were disintegrating into atoms. Then there was blackness.

He could vaguely hear a voice yelling. It sounded like Robert. He was yelling "Medic! Medic! David is down!"

When his eyes fluttered opened, he was lying on the floor in front of his mirror. There was a blanket thrown over the lower part of his body and an army doctor was shining something in his eyes.

"He's OK," the doctor said. "At least I think he is."

"I'm OK," David said, trying to sit up. "I think I just fainted and pulled back through the mirror."

"You sure you're OK?" Robert asked.

"I'm not hurt," David replied. "At least not physically or permanently. It's not something I would want to go through regularly, but it looks like it didn't actually hurt me."

Lieutenant Anderson burst through the door. "Are you OK?" he asked excitedly.

"Yeah," David answered, "but that sucks."

"Sorry about that," he answered, "but this wonderful! As a temporary measure, the data vault can operate in total darkness with the operators wearing virtual reality glasses to act as monitors. For additional security, they can use noise cancelling so the operators voice can't be heard. They can institute that immediately."

"They have to be able to get to total darkness," David said. "And those goggles will have to seal to the face. Even at one percent I could still see pretty clearly. I probably could have read anything that was on Harold's desk. And I was able to walk around just fine. It wasn't until the room went completely dark that I started having trouble."

There was a light knocking at the door. Kong Ling stuck her head in and said, "Kong Jing wants to see that David is actually OK."

"Do you want to get dressed first?" Robert asked.

David looked at him with arched eyebrows. "There are no clothes in the mirror, remember?" he said.

"But that's the mirror," Robert replied. "This is flesh and blood."

"OK," David said, "hand me my robe."

He had just pulled it around himself when Chi ran from the doorway and wrapped her arms around him. She said something which David could not understand.

Kong Ling translated from the doorway. "She says that she was afraid that you had died. She felt you calling out to her, but she couldn't go to you. It was as if there was an impenetrable wall keeping her out."

David held Chi as she cried softly. Turning to Harold, he said, "There is a second test you didn't realize you were doing. Chi couldn't come into the totally dark room even though there is a strong connection between her and me."

Mark and General Crossford were now in the room. "I think that's enough for this morning," Mark said. "I know it takes something out of you to go into the mirror and right now you look like you were rode hard and put away wet."

Kong Ling looked at him and raised her hands as if

asking a question. "American idiom," Robert said quickly. "It refers to putting a horse back in the barn without using a curry comb to rub off the mud and sweat. In other words, David here looks like hell."

Kong Ling smiled at him and immediately began translating for Chi.

"If you could figure out how the mirror translates stuff and duplicate it," Robert said to David, "you could make a billion."

"I'm just glad it does," David answered. "I'm trying to learn Chinese, but it's all Greek to me."

Robert just laughed and said, "I'd love to hear how Momma Ling translates that one."

"Do what you need to do to recover," General Crossford said. Then she asked, "Will you still be able to tour the facility this afternoon?"

David nodded. Then after a moment he asked, "Will some of the rooms be dark?"

"Possibly," the general replied. "Should we make sure all lights are on?"

"No," answered David, "we might see if we can push through into darkness if it isn't 100% dark. And even if it is, it looks like I can stand it for a couple minutes."

"Don't do anything weird," Robert said.

David looked at him and said, "I'm a mirror-walker. We are currently a hundred feet or so underground in an abandoned copper mine trying to come up with a way to detect or defend against an unknown number of invisible enemies. Just what do you consider weird?"

Robert's voice became unusually soft as he answered, "What I mean is, don't take any stupid chances. Keep yourself safe. A lot depends on you."

"I know," David answered. "I know."

Chapter Eight
A Message in a Mirror

For David and Chi it was like having an afternoon off together. They had agreed to meet at the experimentation room at exactly one o'clock, or as Lieutenant Anderson called it, "thirteen hundred hours." For some reason, Chi had far less trouble adjusting to military time than David.

"Stay awake," David said to Robert as he prepared to go into the mirror.

"Around you," Robert replied, "something always happens to keep me wide awake."

"Not today," David replied. "I'm just going for a stroll with my... friend."

"Yeah... yeah," Robert answered as David concentrated on looking into his own left eye. A breath or two to help him relax was all it took before he was pulled into the mirror.

Chi hadn't appeared yet, so David walked around the room inspecting the new equipment that had been set up.

"That must be for tomorrow morning," Chi said softly from behind him.

She walked around in front of him and said with a slightly shaky voice. "You scared me this morning. I thought you had been drawn into the Place of Fire."

"No," David answered. "It was more like being sucked up in a tornado. I think my mirror self was just pulled apart or something."

"I think your mirror self died," Chi said. Her voice was shaking as she spoke. "But for some reason it didn't kill your body. I need to ask Mamma Ling how my mother actually died in the mirror and if she knows how

Chou destroyed her killer."

"Do you want to go back and ask her now?" David asked.

Chi looked down at the floor, sighed, and then looked back up at him. "No," she said, "I would like to ask her privately."

She reached out, took his hand, and said, "Promise me that you will not watch over me tonight. I don't want you to hear what Mamma Ling tells me."

A very weak smile crossed her face. She gave another deep sigh and said, "I think she can sense when you are present. I know she senses me when I walk in the mirror. She might not tell me everything if she thinks you are there."

David just nodded his head.

"Well," he said after a short pause, "we have some exploring to do. Where do you want to start?"

"Let's see what is behind these rooms," Chi said as she began to push through the back wall of the room.

David followed her. The wall was thin and very easy to push through. There was a space behind the wall which was dark, but not DARK. Both David and Chi were able to see fairly well in the extremely dim light.

"Why do you think it is that we can see when there is almost no light?" David asked.

"In the mirror," Chi answered, "you are not seeing with just your eyes, but with your whole body. At least that is what Grandfather always told me."

She stopped and looked slightly upward as memories of her grandfather filled her mind, "Chou often would tell me," she said, "to look at the world with my whole body and not just my eyes. I never understood what he meant until I went into the mirror."

She turned to face him in the tight space. "Sometimes when I am in the mirror, I can see flashes of what is behind me... or beneath my feet."

David paused as if thinking, "I hadn't realized that before," he said, "but yes, when I am in the mirror, it is as if I am looking at the world with my whole body."

He then began to push his arm into the rock wall. "I think this is solid," he said. "... a part of the original mine walls. I doubt we could go very far through that."

They followed the small space along the outside of the rooms, occasionally having to push through wooden or steel braces which held the inner wall in place. Every so often, David would again test how difficult it was to push his arm into the rock wall. After a while he asked Chi, "Where do you think we are?"

"Perhaps approaching the end of the bubble," Chi answered softly. There was caution, but not fear in her voice.

"Then maybe it is time to get back into the light," David answered as he pushed through the inner wall. "Our bubbles will reform if there is a mirror surface nearby and someone we can home in on."

Chi followed right behind him. They were now in a guard room of some sort. There were banks of video monitors along one wall with at least a half-dozen men and women in army uniforms sitting at a long table in front of them. David and Chi walked along the narrow aisleway glancing at the monitors as they walked past.

"That's you," David said suddenly, pointing at one of the monitors. The camera was obviously in the ceiling of Chi's mirror room and was pointed at her from behind.

"There is probably one in your mirror room also," Chi said.

"So much for personal privacy," David answered. His tone of voice clearly express his anger.

At the end of the long table was a desk sitting at right angles to the rest of the monitors. A large monitor split into four images was mounted in front of, and slightly above, the desk. All four images seemed to be of empty areas.

"That's the mantrap room," David said, pointing at the upper right image. "And so is this," now pointing at the lower right image.

"That one is outside the outer door," Chi said pointing to the upper left image.

"And that one," said David, pointing to the lower left image, "must be aimed at the mirror in the mantrap room."

A young man sat at the desk, intently watching the large monitor.

David looked over at Chi and laughed slightly. "Let's conduct an experiment of our own and let them know what we think of them watching us," he said angrily. He then leaned in close and whispered something to Chi. She giggled and held her hands in front of her mouth. Then she nodded her head and took David's hand as they pushed through the wall into the mantrap room itself.

A few moments later, Robert keyed his intercom, "I've got something weird happening," he said. A little excitement was showing in his voice.

"So do I," Kong Ling said. Her voice, as usual, masked any emotion.

"What is it?" a strong female voice asked.

"Well," Robert replied, "it's hard to explain. David came back for just a second... I can tell by his breathing. Then he held both arms up in front of himself and went back into the mirror."

"Kong Jing did the same thing," Kong Ling added.

"And..." Robert continued, "he was flipping the bird with both hands." He paused for just a moment and then said, "Momma Ling, that means he was holding up the middle finger on both hands."

"I know what it means," she answered in her flat

55

tone. Her voice became slightly louder, however, indicating that perhaps she was hiding anger as she added, "Kong Jing did the same thing."

Another voice came on the line. It was Harold, and he was laughing. "I think they have been in the guard room or the mantrap room itself," he said, still laughing.

"If so, they might have projected directly into the mantrap through the mirror," Robert suggested.

Harold paused for a moment and then added, "I'm reviewing images from the mirror that the computer flagged."

"Yes!" he exclaimed. "Both of them appear for just a frame or two in the high-speed camera capture, and both of them are giving us the all-American salute."

"Lieutenant Anderson," Robert said sharply, "is there something out there... perhaps in the guard room that would have upset David or Chi?"

"Yes, there is!" a third voice barked. It was General Crossford. "I am being told it is a programming glitch. I can't prove otherwise, but as soon as they are out of the mirrors, a technician will physically disable the cameras in their mirror rooms or permanently turn them away from the mirrors.

"Kong Ling," she continued, "I officially apologize on behalf of my staff and my government for this intrusion into Kong Jing's personal space. I assure you that all recordings from that camera will be deleted."

The general was speaking from the guard room where she had run as soon as Robert had indicated that something was happening. Unknown to her, David and Chi were standing close behind her as she yelled at the guards for having pulled up and then recorded the feed from Chi's mirror room. Several times Chi turned to David and said, "Her words don't make any sense."

"Idioms," David replied. "Good old-fashioned American cuss words strung together in one of the longest and most vehement dressing-downs that I have ever seen or heard."

"David and Chi, if you are here," Lieutenant Anderson said from the small desk in the corner of the room, "I want to thank you for testing our high-speed detection system." He looked around the room, not sure whether or not he was speaking to anyone and continued. "I'm pretty sure the big brass are going to want to see these images. I will blur out things to preserve your modesty, but there is no way I cannot send these pictures up the chain of command."

His comments also went out over the intercom, and Robert spoke up. "Blur out the faces also," he said forcefully. "We have no way of knowing who is actually looking at those pics and David and Chi are in enough danger already."

"That's an order," General Crossford said sharply. Her microphone had not been on during her tirade, but evidently she was still monitoring the line. "And Lieutenant Anderson, I want the original images encrypted so no one but you and I can open those files. You can give me the password for the file later."

"Yes, Ma'am," Harold answered. He then looked almost exactly where David and Chi were standing and shrugged his shoulders. He made sure his intercom mic was off and then said softly, "Best I could do."

"He can sense us," Chi said excitedly. "He knew where we were standing."

"It could have just been a good guess," David said slowly. "Or perhaps when I overlapped him it created a connection of some sort."

He turned to Chi and said, "There is so much about the mirror world that I don't understand."

He paused and continued, "For example, the bubble. We know it is bigger outside than underground, and it is bigger when two of us form it. But can we

57

affect that bubble? Can we make it bigger or smaller?"

As he spoke, he moved his arms out to express bigger and pulled them in to express smaller. As he pulled his arms close to his body, Chi screamed.

"What happened?!" he cried out.

"The bubble collapsed," Chi said. Her face showed her fear. "For a moment, I was partially in the Place of Fire. Then I yelled, 'Bigger!' as loud as I could and the bubble moved back out."

"I didn't mean to collapse the bubble," David said.

"You didn't know you could move the bubble," Chi said forcefully. "So in your ignorance, you did move it."

"And I almost put you in the Place of Fire," David said. Now it was his face that showed fear. "I wonder what else I don't know about the mirror that might harm you... or me."

Chi looked at David almost blankly. Then she said flatly, "Chou always said, 'The difference between the Master and the Novice is that the Master knows that he does not know.'"

"Well," David responded, "I know that there are many things that I will never know about the mirror."

"I think it is time to return," Chi said. "Momma Ling will worry if I am too long in the mirror." She giggled and said, "And besides, projecting an exact form while I came through the mirror was very difficult and exhausting."

"But it was worth it, wasn't it?" David said, almost giggling himself.

"I will see you at dinner," Chi said. Then she shimmered and disappeared.

"One more thing I have to test," David said aloud to himself. He then walked over to the edge of Harold's desk and shouted, "Lieutenant Harold Tecumseh Anderson. Can you hear me?"

The Lieutenant's head spun toward David's voice.

"David?" he asked. "Is there a problem?"

David took a deep breath as he stepped away from the mirror. "Robert," he called out, "please tell Lieutenant Anderson that I was just checking to see if he could hear me."

"O... K..." Robert answered slowly as he picked up the intercom. "Lieutenant Anderson," he began, "I have no idea what this means, but David says he was just checking to see if you could hear him."

"Thank you," Harold replied. As he shut off the intercom, he took a deep breath and stared off across the room, as if lost in thought.

Chapter Nine
Another Morning Meeting

The conference room meeting the next morning began with another apology from General Crossford for the video surveillance in the mirror room. "I assure you," she said firmly, "that it will never happen again."

Chi said, "Thank you," as soon as Kong Ling translated. It was one of a growing list of English words and phrases that she was learning.

David smiled and said, "I doubt the technicians responsible will forget your comments for a long, long time."

"You were there?" the general asked.

"Yes," David answered.

"Good!" she replied firmly. "Then you know that I meant what I said. ... And I sincerely apologize for something which happened under my command."

"Before we talk about today's tests," Mark interjected, "let's discuss what we learned yesterday."

He looked down at his notes and said, "First off, and this is very important, the high-speed cameras can detect a mirror-walker entering a room."

"If..." Robert said brusquely, "the camera is pointed at the right shiny surface and has a boatload of computer stuff analyzing the images."

Mark looked over at his brother. "I didn't say it was a perfect solution," he said testily. "I said it can be done."

He took a deep breath and said, "We also learned that a mirror-walker cannot stay in a totally dark environment, and I don't mean dim, I mean *TOTALLY* dark."

"It kills them," David said flatly.

When everyone looked at him in surprise, he

continued, "The mirror self ceases to exist... disintegrates... is pulled apart when trapped in total darkness. That is death. The darkness kills the mirror-walker self but somehow I was able to return to my flesh self."

He looked around the table and then paused to look directly at Chi. "It's not something I would want to go through again," he said, "but it doesn't really damage me... and I was able to go back into the mirror later."

"Anything else?" Mark asked.

Again it was David who spoke up. "Yes," he said slowly. "Harold can hear me when I'm in the mirror."

"No, I can't," Lieutenant Anderson quickly replied, "I've never heard you while you were in the mirror."

"You turned to face me when I called out to you and you asked if I was all right," David said firmly.

"But I didn't hear you," he replied. "I just... just... knew you were there and trying to contact me." He swallowed and said softly, "I thought you were in trouble."

"And Chi says that I can hear her," Kong Ling said. "I think that if there is a close connection of some sort other people can sense when the person who is walking in the mirror is near them."

"Noted," said General Crossford, pointing to the recording device sitting on the table.

She nodded at Mark and he said, "Today we are going to see if we can create a black space that isn't black."

"There is one more thing before that," Kong Ling said as she rose slowly from her chair. She pointed to one of the guards standing behind her and he sat down in her chair as she moved to the open end of the table. "He will translate for Kong Jing so she knows what I am saying."

She took a deep breath and said, "Last night Kong

61

Jing asked me for details about her mother's death and the death of the mirror-walker who killed her. I have tried for many years to forget my husband's words as he told me what happened, but the lives of my Chi and her Beloved may depend on them knowing what happened."

"'Beloved' is what Chi calls me in the mirror," David said sheepishly. "I think Mamma Ling is emphasizing that this is important to our mirror selves."

"It is important to all of us," Kong Ling said firmly.

She then smoothed the front of her blouse and said softly, "My husband was a Master of the Mirror. My son and daughter were also able to go into themselves and walk in the mirrors. He taught them the proper ways of the mirror. There were a few other mirror-walkers that he discovered and trained. He wanted to use the power of the mirror for good, but corrupt members of our government attempted to take control. They wanted to use the power of the mirror for their own evil purposes.

"My husband, of course, refused to cooperate. My son and daughter also refused– as did almost all the others. But there was one mirror-walker who did not. He was, himself, evil and relished the idea of doing evil things in the mirror. He and some corrupt members of our government devised a plan. One by one, those who had refused were tricked into a mirror bubble where this evil beast could attack them. He caught my beloved Kong Li by surprise and threw her outside the bubble into the Place of Chaos and Fire."

It was obvious that she was holding back a sob as she said, "That is the only way to truly kill a mirror-walker."

She straightened her back and said, "But Kong Li was not alone in the mirror. My son, Kong Wei was with her. He saw what happened and thought that he could save her. He crossed the barrier into the Place of Chaos where he also died."

Her head drooped and she said softly, "I have learned since then that even though he defeated one of the Fire Warriors, all that happened was that he replaced his conquest and became a Fire Warrior himself. He could not save Kong Li and now he cannot save himself. One day he will be defeated and then it will be his time to go into the pit of fire."

She stood silently, breathing deeply, for a long time, then she continued. "My husband was a gentle man, but he knew that this evil beast had to be stopped. The other mirror-walker accepted his challenge and met him at the same place where Kong Li and Kong Wei had been destroyed."

She smiled at David and then at Chi and said, "The greatest weakness of evil men is pride. They think they are better and more skilled than anyone else. And if they are young and the other is old, they have even more contempt in their hearts for the other's skills."

She paused and took another deep breath before continuing. "Age means less in the mirror," she said flatly. "And my husband had studied many of the ancient books and scrolls on the art of weaponless war. The evil beast let my husband walk into the same trap he had prepared for Kong Li, but my husband was ready for him. The fight was long and bloody. They were both very powerful. So powerful that the effects of the fight itself seeped over into the real world. I could see bite marks and scratches appear on my husband's body as he stood in front of his mirror. Finally my husband collapsed and lay bleeding on the floor in front of his mirror.

"He pushed himself to his feet and said, 'It is finished. I took him to the Place of Chaos.'"

She took a long, deep breath and finished. "He never said anything else about the fight. But that the was last time that he went into the mirror to do anything but visit the place where his ancestral village once stood."

She smiled slightly. "He said he found it peaceful there." She smiled again and said, "That is where he met David."

Kong Ling walked silently back to her seat. The guard quickly returned to his place and she sat down. As soon as she had pulled her chair back up to the table, she said, "So now you know how to kill a mirror-walker. There is only one way. And that is for another mirror-walker to push them into the Place of Chaos and Fire. There, the Dogs of Chaos and the Fire Warriors will destroy their mirror selves... and their real bodies will die."

After a long silence, Mark spoke up. "Kong Ling," he said softly, "I am very sorry that you had to bring all of this back up, but we needed to know."

"My husband," Kong Ling replied, "was hoping he was truly the last mirror-walker. He was afraid that with all our new technology, governments would figure out how to use the mirror for warfare."

"I wish I could say that would never happen," General Crossford said slowly, "but the reality of the world is that whoever has the best toys wins. We have to explore everything as a possible weapon of defense."

"Idioms don't translate well," David said quickly.

"I understand," Kong Ling said in her emotionless voice. "There is a similar idiom in Chinese... and probably every other language on earth."

"Our problem right now," Mark said, trying to regain control of the meeting, "is that we have to stop one rogue mirror-walker from stealing secrets and sowing havoc all over the world. We know that a mirror-walker can't work in complete darkness, but what about if it is totally dark and us humans... I mean flesh selves... are using night-vision systems of some sort. Could we then create an area where fleshies could work, but mirror-walkers couldn't?"

"How are you going to test that?" David asked.

"It's really simple," Harold replied. "We dim the room to almost darkness and then use the same frequency laser illuminators that are used in various night-vision systems to put numbers up on the wall. You walk through and report back what numbers you were able to see."

"That sounds pretty simple," Robert said. "It's going to be an easy morning for David."

"This afternoon, we have something not quite so easy," Mark replied. "We are going to try every type of detection device we can think of to see if anything gets triggered by a mirror-walker."

"Let's leave this afternoon for this afternoon and concentrate on the task at hand," General Crossford said as she stood up. "This meeting is adjourned. David and Kong Jing, please report to your mirror rooms."

She paused and said, "And I assure you that the video systems in those rooms have been disabled."

Mark spoke quickly before either David or Chi could leave. "Same procedure as yesterday. David will be our primary test subject. Chi will be watching for intruders and letting us know if anything hinky happens."

***

About fifteen minutes later, Robert reported over the intercom system, "David is in the mirror."

Shortly thereafter Kong Ling's voice said, "Kong Jing has become Chi."

A few more minutes later, Mark spoke to the spot where David and Chi were supposed to be. Chi was standing on the taped 'X' on the floor as instructed. David was standing behind Mark studying the various laser projectors.

"David," Mark began, "all you need to do is go into the other room where we have the lighting at one percent and read any numbers you see on the wall. We also want you to slowly step through the laser projectors and tell us if any of them seem to illuminate your skin in any way. That would be an indication that lasers might be able to be used in a detection system."

He waited a moment and then said. "I am assuming you heard and understood all of that, so I am dimming the lights and turning on the laser projectors."

The lights in the other room went dim. To the technicians sitting in the observation room, it appeared that the test room was now dark. Several of the techs put on different forms of night-vision goggles and began making adjustments to the laser projectors, focusing the numbers on the opposite wall of the test room.

David stepped into the test room walking very slowly as he looked for any hint of light on his skin. He was moving very carefully, and not just so he could carefully examine his skin for light. There was that very slight chance that the laser light, though low power, could be dangerous to his mirror self. There was no real way of knowing... yet.

He could see two numbers on the wall of the room. One was a brownish-looking five. The other was a bright, almost red, seven. When he reached the end of the room, he pulled back out of the mirror and told Robert what he had seen.

Robert relayed the information through the intercom. As he was speaking, Kong Ling joined the conversation with a slight laugh. "I know you were using only David," she said, "but Kong Jing also read the numbers. Except she saw a blue four and a turquoise nine."

Robert now laughed. "I guess you are going to have

to repeat all tests," he said, "once with David and once with Chi."

"No need," Mark said dejectedly. "We don't have the rogue here to test what lasers he can't see. He can probably see the two and the six. That cancels out the rest of this morning."

Lieutenant Anderson summed it up for everyone when he said, "Well, to quote Thomas Edison, we now know another thing what won't work. Maybe the tests this afternoon will show us something that will work."

Chapter Ten
Two of Six

That afternoon, when David went into the mirror and came out in the test room, the layout of the room had been changed. Rather than a big, open room, it was now made into almost a maze by office cubicle partitions set up throughout the room. David debated whether he should just walk straight through the short walls to the other side of the room, but Mark's voice came over the speakers.

"We want you to walk up and down each of the corridors while the detectors scan the area," Mark explained. "We want to see if there is anything that might detect you."

Lieutenant Anderson quickly added, "When you get to the end of the zig-zags turn around and go back. We will be increasing the sensitivity of the detectors until they eventually go off continually from random background noise."

David knew that they couldn't hear him, but he still called back, "I hope there is at least a hunk of cheese at the end of this laboratory maze."

After what seemed like a hundred trips up and down the tiny corridors formed by the cubicle walls, Mark once again spoke up. "I've instructed Chi to join you," he said. "We have everything set just below where they started to show something. Maybe they will trigger if there are two of you."

This time there were only a dozen or so trips back and forth in the maze before Mark said, "David and Chi, I think we all need to meet in the conference room to discuss these results. Please meet us there as soon as you are dressed."

David arrived a few minutes later wrapped in his

robe. Chi was fully dressed when she entered the small conference room.

General Crossford started the short meeting with a question. "What did we learn?" she asked brusquely.

Lieutenant Harold Anderson spoke up first. "David triggered three of the nineteen detectors," he said while shaking his head slowly. "So did Chi, but we had to have the sensitivity so far up that it would be popping off every time there was a lightning strike a hundred miles away. At those settings all of the detectors were triggering regularly just because of the background noise."

Special Agent Mark Nash waited for Harold to finish before saying, "Too many false positives are as bad as no detection at all."

"What about you?" the general asked, directing the question to David. "Did you feel anything?"

"No, not really," David replied. "I didn't feel anything or see any light on my skin or anything like that. But I was starting to feel like Colonel Zelko. I was sure I was invisible, but I was still waiting for the missiles to hit."

Everyone but General Crossford looked at him with wide, questioning eyes. "I can only hope that is the case," she said. Then turning to the rest of the table, she explained. "Young Mister Malone has once again shown that he is a military history buff. Lieutenant Colonel Dale Zelko was the pilot of a F-117 stealth fighter which was shot down in Serbia back in '99. They used a really old-fashioned long wave radar that could detect that there was something there, but not really 'see' anything else about it. They coupled it with a modern high-frequency unit, which is what the stealth technology works best against. If the long wave said something was there, but the short wave said there wasn't, then they knew they were pinging a stealth fighter. They just kept roughly tracking it with the long wave until he opened his bomb bay doors and lost the stealth effect."

"Wait a minute!" Lieutenant Anderson said. "What if we did that?"

"Used old-fashioned radar?" Robert asked.

"No," Harold quickly replied. "What if we use multiple detectors at the same time all set to very high sensitivity. Six should do it. Two of them could be the two that best detected David. The other four would be ones that never blipped for him. If all six blip, it's lightning or a passing train or whatever. But if *ONLY* the two Ghost Busters ping, then it's a mirror-walker."

"How long would it take to set something like that up for testing?" General Crossford asked.

"We can be ready with a rough test in about fifteen minutes," Harold answered excitedly. "There's already a computer program which displays responses from the detectors and presents them on the screen. All we have to do is tweak that program so it works in real time and presents the activity of all six detectors at the same time."

He paused and said, "We can work out algorithms for a system later, but for now, the human eye can tell noise from intruder."

The lieutenant immediately left the room.

"Detection is just the first step," Mark said.

"But it is a very big step," Kong Ling said. "Darkness and removal of all reflective surfaces can help deter intrusion," she continued in her perfectly calm voice, "but eventually there must also be detection and destruction. My husband's worst nightmares will become reality. Unseen armies will fight each other to the death in the mirrors of the world."

"And..." David began. He seemed to be at a loss for words, or perhaps he was just having trouble giving voice to what he knew had to be said. Finally, he took a

70

deep breath and looked around the table before beginning. "And now that the governments of the world know that such a thing as a mirror-walker exists they will start testing people. They will start with members of their armies, but soon every child will be set down in front of a mirror and asked to look into themselves and think of their parents in the next room or whatever. If the child gives any indication of being pulled into the mirror, or if an improved version of Harold's detector goes off in the next room, the child will be the property of the state from then on."

"I wish I could say that would never happen," Mark said flatly.

"I wish I could say that it isn't already being planned," General Crossford said. There was true regret in her voice. She looked over at David and said, "We have honored our promise not to use you, but we have begun the search for other mirror-walkers. And yes, we plan to start with current members of the military." She paused and then added, "I hope it never comes down to putting children in front of the mirror."

"But it will," David said.

"Yes, it will." Kong Ling replied. There was obvious emotion in her voice and it was raspy. A tear flowed down her cheek. "And other mothers," she continued, "will have to watch their children's bodies die after their mirror selves have been destroyed in the Place of Chaos."

She bowed her head, crying softly. The room remained silent until Lieutenant Anderson called on the intercom and said, "We're ready to test."

"David and Kong Jing," Mark said quietly, "I want you both to come directly into the test room. Walk through the area... sometimes together... sometimes separated by a slight distance... sometimes at opposite ends of the room. I want to see if these detectors can tell that there are two of you."

Ten minutes later, Mark and General Crossford stood anxiously behind Lieutenant Anderson as he watched a large monitor screen. "We have four detector areas," he explained, pointing to the screen which was divided into quadrants. "That's all we could set up for now, but they cover a pretty large area of the room and will act as a feasibility test. There are six detectors in each of the four areas. The background detectors will show as green or blue. The two we're hoping will detect David will show as red and orange."

As if to prove his statement, six colored bars rose up in each quadrant. They weren't exactly the same height, but they did rapidly rise and then slowly fall together. "That's definitely background noise of some sort," he said calmly. "I think," he added a little less calmly.

Then two of the bars suddenly peaked in the lower left quadrant. One was red, the other was orange. The green and blue bars remained at a low level.

"That could be a mirror-walker," he said excitedly. After just a few seconds, the red and orange bars in that quadrant dropped back to a low bobbing level equal to the others, but the corresponding bars in the upper right quadrant now towered over the green and blue bars.

"He's moving into section three," Harold said calmly.

"Wait a minute!" he suddenly cried out. "We've got activity in section one again."

"That can't be right," he muttered to himself as he stared intently at the screen and checked readings on some of the nearby equipment. After a few moments he turned to Mark with a grin. "Chi's not in here watching, is she?" he asked.

"Nope," Mark replied. "I told her to stroll around over there with David. Sort of a blind test of the system."

"Well," General Crossford said with a satisfied smile, "I think we have a possible detection system that can be set up rather quickly at sensitive spots."

"David and Chi," Mark called out loudly, "come back out of the mirrors and meet us back in the conference room."

Another ten minutes passed before everyone was back in the conference room. Lieutenant Anderson was hardly able to contain himself. "If we can detect you with this crude equipment," he almost shouted, "just think what could be done with a little engineering."

He waved his hands in the air, "A few tweaks and we could have real-time maps indicating possible mirror-walkers. We could use directed beams and even paint an image of the mirror-walker himself... or herself."

"Or there could be some mirror-walkers who are invisible to the system," David said slowly.

"That, too," Harold said. "But they could be detected by mirror-walker patrols."

David took a deep breath and said softly, "So it begins."

"Yes," General Crossford answered. "So it begins."

She then turned to Harold and said, "Lieutenant Anderson, while the rest of the team enjoys some time off this evening, I would like you to get your preliminary findings into an official report. By the end of the day tomorrow we will have defense contractors working twenty-four/seven developing suitable systems based on your findings."

Kong Ling coughed slightly and General Crossford added, "Make sure that the report is also forwarded to the Chinese authorities."

She then turned back to David and said, "We may need you and Kong Jing for some occasional testing, but it is looking like we can now turn our efforts to our number two priority– finding our rogue mirror-walker."

Addressing the rest of the table she said, "But for tonight, let's celebrate this victory... except for Lieutenant Anderson, of course, who will be busy writing his report. We can discuss what our next steps should be in the morning."

Chapter Eleven
Intruder

The mood in the lounge after supper was very relaxed. Several of the techs and guards were watching television. A few were playing cards. Mark and General Crossford were sitting quietly discussing sports teams. Kong Ling, David, Kong Jing, and Robert were sitting at a small card table. Momma Ling had suggested that she teach David a Chinese dice game. The facility was pretty well stocked with various types of games to pass the time once the snows accumulated topside so there was more than the needed number of dice and dice cups.

"This is a pretty simple game," she said, "and you can use hand gestures to indicate what you are saying, so it will allow you and Kong Jing to interact in the real world."

"Both worlds are real!" David immediately said–more loudly and more heatedly than he had truly intended. His voice softened and he said, "I'm sorry. It's just that people keep thinking that the mirror world is only make-believe. It's not all fairy tales and magic rainbows."

"You don't have to tell me," Momma Ling replied. "I have lost two children to the mirror world."

David immediately repeated his, "I'm sorry," but Kong Ling held up her hand and said, "No need to apologize. You understand my pain... I understand your anger. But the term you use... flesh world... means something else in Chinese. I believe it would translate back into English as the world of porn. Obviously saying real world carries additional meaning in English... or at least for you."

David laughed slightly. "That is one great advantage of the mirror. There is no need of translation–

though idioms still don't make sense."

"This game is very simple," Kong Ling said, returning to her goal of a relaxing evening together. "But I think you both will enjoy it"

The game was called "Liar's Dice." Kong Ling also gave the Chinese name, "shuōhu ng zhě de sh izi," but it meant nothing to David. Once she handed out the dice cups and the five dice, however, Robert said, "This looks like the dice game from that pirate movie." He then used a horrible impersonation of a pirate to say, "Twelve Fives."

Kong Ling laughed lightly. She was very pretty when she laughed. Then she said, "Yes, Mister Nash, it is the game from that pirate movie. Only they didn't invent it for the movie. It has been a drinking and betting game in China for many centuries."

She was about to explain how the game was played, when Lieutenant Anderson's voice came over the intercom. "May I have your attention, please? Would technicians Beloved and Chi please report to the guard room to have their visitors' passes validated for tomorrow. Technicians David and Kong Jing, you don't need to be alarmed. Your passes are still good. Thank you."

Everyone in the room froze and then looked rapidly to General Crossford. "No action... yet," she said tersely. "Lieutenant Anderson thinks we have a visitor and he wants a mirror-walker to verify. ... He also wants no visible or audible alarms."

She pointed at Robert and David and then at Kong Ling and Kong Jing and indicated that they should go. The direction she was pointing was toward the mirror rooms.

She then pointed at the Marine guards and then the Chinese Security people and then at herself to indicate that they should follow her.

As they hurried down the hallway, Robert said, "He asked specifically for the mirror-walkers." Then he added quickly. "But he asked in a way that sounds like he thinks he is being overheard."

"Or watched," Kong Ling said flatly as she closed the door to Chi's mirror room.

David quickly stripped off his clothes and stood in front of the black mirror saying softly aloud, "Guard Room, Guard Room, Guard Room."

Almost as soon as he stepped into the room, he was driven back by a heavy blow to the center of his chest by a dark-haired man who looked like he would be more comfortable on the steppes of eastern Russia. At least that's what David thought in the brief second he could see the man's face before the intruder's head crashed into his stomach.

"It was the eyes," he thought to himself, remembering a paper he had done in college on the Volga Tatars. Many of the people from that border area between Russia and China have traces of Mongol heritage... which shows primarily in the shape of their eyes.

He didn't have much time to think further about it because the intruder was driving him backwards through the wall into the mantrap area. He wasn't sure how, but he could feel the boundary pulling in toward him as he was being pushed back. It wasn't just that he was near the boundary of his bubble. The rogue mirror-walker was manipulating the bubble to make it smaller. If he couldn't break free from the intruder's grip, he would soon be thrown through the boundary into the Place of Fire.

He could feel the darkness approaching when suddenly the intruder's body shook and his face contorted with surprise. Chi, screaming and yelling, had launched herself in a flying kick at the back of his head.

The intruder released David and spun to face Chi. What followed looked like a badly-choreographed scene from a grade B action movie. If everything weren't so deadly real, David would have laughed as both Chi and the intruder thrust and kicked and blocked each other's moves, grunting loudly with each attempted blow.

In a movie, the good guy– or gal– would always win, but this was real life, and the intruder was more skilled at the martial arts than Chi was and outweighed her by almost half. Chi was knocked across the room by a well-placed kick to her side. Then the intruder turned his fury back at David. To his surprise, David was able to temporarily fend off the obviously very well-trained attacker. Then Chi came rushing back to the fight.

David could see the boundary suddenly rush in just as the intruder placed a well-aimed kick squarely in the middle of Chi's chest. She fell backward and would have surely fallen through into the blackness, but David suddenly threw his arms outward and yelled, "Bigger!"

The intruder's expression of shock as the boundary returned to its normal size and considerably beyond was short-lived. He turned and advanced now toward David.

"So you want to do this the hard way," he said coarsely as he warily moved closer to David while keeping an eye on Chi who lay gasping on the floor.

He seemed to be toying with David. Perhaps he knew that David's fighting skills were minimal. Perhaps he was making sure that he did not expose his back to Chi, who was back on her feet and seemed to be recovering. Or perhaps he was just waiting for the right moment when everyone was in exactly the right place so he could launch a quick, brutal kick to the side of David's head followed by a rapid series of kicks driving Chi back once again through the shrinking boundary.

David heard Chi scream as she fell backward through the boundary. If his head had been clear he would never have done it, but his mind was still fogged from the force of the intruder's blow. Without thinking of what it was he was doing, he thought– or perhaps said out loud, "Place of Fire!"

He immediately found himself on the other side of the boundary in the darkness with the Dogs of Chaos and the Fire Warriors. The dogs were not snarling at him, though. In fact they stood around him looking confused– almost afraid.

Looking down at his body, David could see that there was a bubble around him, but it was tight to his body almost like an invisible suit of armor. The dogs were now staying well back from him. Evidently they were unsure of this strange figure who was before them, but not really in the Place of Fire.

Looking across the darkness, David could see Chi lying crumpled on the ground. The Fire Warriors had already driven her close to the edge of the pit of fire. One of them approached him and spoke. He recognized the voice of Uncle Wei from the first time he was in the Place of Chaos and Fire. Wei said, "You are truly a Master of the Mirror if you can come to the Place of Fire in this way."

He looked back and forth between David and Chi and then said, "Because you have brought your mirror bubble with you I cannot attack you, but you still cannot save Chi."

He stood with both swords on the ground and spoke even more loudly. "If you attack me," he said, "your shield of protection will disappear as soon as you touch me."

As Wei was speaking, the hounds moved silently past David and stood with the other Fire Warrior ready to push Chi into the fire. Chi was now standing on the very edge of the pit.

"Chi! Run to me!" David called out.

There was fear, but not panic on her face as she turned to the sound of his voice and ran towards the gap in the circle left by the Fire Warrior who was facing David. That Fire Warrior spun to block her. While he was turning, he swung one of his giant scimitars in a wide arc while bracing his body against the ground with the other.

Chi continued to run toward him. It looked like he would chop her in half as she ran, but at the last moment, she dropped and slid feet first beneath the swinging blade. The Fire Warrior immediately shifted his weight and brought the other scimitar down in a chopping motion trying to stop her. She rolled over as the heavy sword descended toward her neck and cried out as it made contact with her shoulders. She was still screaming as her slide carried her to David's feet.

"Stand up," he said firmly. As she did, David reached out his arms to hold her and his bubble enveloped her. "Home," he thought and suddenly they were both in his living room. Chi was hanging limp in his arms. Blood was running down her side from a gash across the back of her shoulders.

"Mirror room," he shouted at her. "You must go back to Momma Ling." She shimmered in his arms. He felt a strange tingling as she disappeared.

Chapter Twelve
Return to the Fire

As soon as Chi disappeared, David said, "Return!" and found himself standing in front of the black mirror in his mirror room.

Robert was shouting at him, "What the hell happened!? Are you OK!?"

In the distance he could hear alarms sounding and soldiers running. Then he heard a shrill scream. Somehow he knew it was Kong Ling's voice. Her scream faded out and she was now yelling something in Chinese. One of the guards outside her door repeated her cry in English, "Medic! Medic! Kong Jing is down! Kong Jing is down!"

David ran from his room into hers. Chi was face down on the floor in front of her brass mirror. Kong Ling was holding her. There was a large pool of blood on the floor around them.

He ran over to her and took her hand in his. "Chi, can you hear me?" he called out. "Don't die!" he sobbed. "Don't die!"

He felt a hand grip his shoulder, pulling him back. "Let the medics do their job," Robert's voice said softly. As David stood up, Robert slipped the robe over his shoulders. "It looks bad," Robert continued, "but it doesn't look deep. Unless that sword has some magic killing power, she's got a chance."

"No one knows what those swords can do," David said softly. "You are not supposed to be able to come back from there."

"But this is the third time you and Chi have pulled that off," Robert said, holding up his hand with three fingers extended. "If you can do that, you can do almost anything."

81

"Except defeat that rogue mirror-walker," David said bitterly.

There were now four Marines around Chi. "Make a hole!" one of the them yelled and they picked her up. Evidently they had their arms joined under her because they were able to lift her off the ground almost as if she were on a stretcher. "Make a hole!" one of the Marines repeated as they reached the doorway. David, Robert, Kong Ling, and her security detail raced along behind the medics.

David was slightly surprised when at the end of the corridor, they suddenly entered a very well-equipped medical facility. Mark's voice from behind them explained, "When the snows get deep and the blizzards are roaring, you might as well be in Antarctica. They have to be ready for anything down here."

Chi was now face down on an examination table. A sheet had been draped over the lower part of her body. A woman in green surgical scrubs hurriedly thrown over her uniform was examining the wound.

"One major bleeder," she said firmly. She then gave instructions to one of the medics. David couldn't hear what she said, but the medic ran to a tall cupboard and brought back a small, rolled packet. The doctor flipped it open and it unrolled flat on a side table. She then looked at two of the medics and yelled out, "Masks, gloves... and get these other people out of here!"

One of the medics made hand motions indicating that everyone should leave. Once they were standing in the hallway with the door closed to the infirmary, Kong Ling turned to David and said, "She was in the Place of Chaos again! You both were! The only way she could have gotten injured like that is from the sword of a Fire Warrior!" She then started crying quietly.

David looked around at the faces staring at him. General Crossford had now joined them in the hallway.

"The rogue mirror-walker was in the guard room," he began. His voice was soft, flat, and almost devoid of emotion, but his face was contorted with grief and anger. "He attacked me as soon as I stepped through the mirror."

He took a deep breath and his voice became firmer. "He *KNEW* what he was doing. He knew how to kill a mirror-walker. That means he's done it before. And he can control the mirror bubble with just his thoughts. He drew it in close and tried to drive me through the barrier into the darkness."

There was a catch in his voice as he continued, "He might have done it, but Chi hit him like a flying windmill." He smiled as he said, "She's good... but he was better. He got through her defenses and kicked her backwards. It should have driven her through the barrier, but I was able to expand the bubble before she fell through. That surprised him, but not for long."

David took a deep breath. His voice returned closer to normal as he said, "He came back after me, but that was really a feint. He was drawing Chi into a trap. He waited until she was almost upon him and then pulled the bubble in so that it was right next to us. He rang my bell with a kick to the head so I couldn't move the bubble, then he kicked her in the chest several times real fast and she fell backwards through the barrier. After that, he spun and kicked at me again. As I fell backwards, all I could think of was Chi. I intentionally went to the Place of Fire to try to save her."

David laughed and looked Robert in the eyes. His voice sounded oddly high pitched– almost maniacal– as he continued, "I didn't know I could do that. ... I didn't know anybody could do that. ... But I did it. I should have just joined her forever in the pit of fire when he kicked me through the barrier, but because I had been there before and Chi saved me, I was able to return intentionally... and my bubble came with me. It wasn't very big. It was almost like a thick coating around my body, but I was in the Place of Chaos and Fire without really being there."

David was starting to become more agitated as he recounted the events. "The Fire Warriors were driving Chi toward the pit of fire," he said loudly. "I shouted at them and they turned to face me. Uncle Wei told me I couldn't save her. I couldn't interfere... I couldn't stop them because if I attacked him, I would lose my bubble of safety. So I stayed where I was and called on her to run to me."

His voice began to shake as he tried to hold back sobs. "She tried to slide under Wei's sword. I thought she made it, but..."

Kong Ling reached out and pulled him onto her shoulder as he dissolved into tears. She was still holding him tight when the door opened and the doctor stepped into the hallway. Her green scrubs were stained with blood.

"She's going to make it," the doctor said firmly. "She lost a lot of blood, but the injuries are relatively minor. There is no major muscle or tendon damage. Whatever cut her was extremely sharp and very clean. I doubt there will be any infection, but we have given her high levels of antibiotics, just to be sure."

"Can we see her?" Kong Ling asked. Her voice quavered as she spoke. For once, it wasn't possible for her to disguise her emotions.

"We will get her transferred to sick bay, and then you can see her," the doctor answered. "But only close relatives."

"I am her Grandmother," Kong Ling replied. Then pointing to David she said, "And Beloved is her mirror brother."

"And they don't go nowhere without their guards,"

Robert interjected gruffly pointing at himself, the Marine guards, and their Chinese counterpart.

"OK," the doctor said. "The THREE of you can see her in the sick bay shortly. The additional guards can remain at station just outside her door."

***

It was almost a half hour later when Kong Ling and David stood next to Chi's bed. Robert stood back and watched warily, not sure what dangers might be present. The guards stood just as warily right outside the door.

Chi was lying on her stomach on a pile of pillows. Her upper back and shoulders were heavily bandaged. She looked weak. Kong Ling reached out and held her hand. David did the same on the other side of the bed.

"He let me escape," Chi sobbed out. "Even before he became a Fire Warrior Uncle Wei was a master of the sword. No one could just slide under his blade, but I had to try." Sobs broke up her voice as she continued, "The Fire Warrior swung his sword to cut off my head, but the Uncle Wei that is still alive in him somehow held it back."

She clung to David's hand and continued to cry. When her sobs finally eased, she took a deep breath and said softly, but very firmly, "He let me escape. We must save him. Somehow we must save him."

"But first we must save ourselves," David replied. "The warrior in the mirror knows we are a threat to him now. He will not stop until we have been destroyed."

There was a beep and Robert lifted his intercom to his ear. He coughed slightly and said, "I hate to cut this short, but General Crossford wants an immediate conference in the guard room."

"Not the conference room?" David asked.

Robert shrugged and replied, "She said guard

room...and she's the boss, so..."

"Do they need Kong Ling?" David asked.

Robert relayed the question and then said, "Maybe later, but for now, Momma Ling can stay with Chi."

As they left the room, Robert leaned in close and said softly to David, "Did Chi speak to you in English in there just now?"

David shook his head. "No," he replied. "I think the mirror effect is bleeding over... like it did that time back in the van for you." He shrugged. "If you ask Momma Ling, I'm sure she will tell you that Chi was speaking Chinese, but we heard English. Normally that effect lasts only a few seconds once someone comes out of the mirror. I don't know why it held for so long. Maybe it's because she was wounded in the mirror or because we came back from the Place of Fire again. Whatever the reason, it will fade soon."

"There's something very odd about that Place of Fire," Robert said. "When you go there, I can sometimes see it, and not just when you are coming out of the mirror. It's a nasty place. I saw her try to get to you. It looked like the Fire Warrior thing got her as she tried to slide under his sword. I wasn't sure if either of you was coming back."

David started laughing.

"What's so funny?" Robert asked, almost angrily.

"There was a time you called me a nut job for just talking about the mirror," David said, "and now you are saying that the Place of Fire is odd." He laughed again. "Does that mean that all the rest of this is normal?"

"Amazing what weird shit you get used to," Robert replied, "ain't it?"

Chapter Thirteen
To Catch a Spy

When Robert and David arrived at the guard room, Mark, General Crossford, and Lieutenant Anderson were standing around a desk, bent over, looking at a monitor.

"Evidently they come in through the best mirror surface nearest the target," Harold was saying. "And I had a high-speed camera aimed at the mirror in front of my desk. I was trying to sync it to the detectors to see if we could capture anything once they triggered."

"So did you get anything when the detectors went off?" David asked.

Harold pointed to a smear on the monitor and then quickly pressed some buttons to back up the recording. There was an image on only five frames of the high-speed recording. The first and fifth images were just slight blurs. The second and fourth images looked more like a human shadow. The center image, however, very clearly showed the face of a man with very dark hair and almost black eyes that had a pronounced almond shape.

"That camera was recording at a thousand frames a second," he said emphatically. "That means he was visible to the camera for only a little more than a millisecond."

"But I could see Chi when she came through my bathroom mirror last year," Robert said.

"And I saw him," Harold said, pointing at the screen, "when he came through the monitor screen at Shangri-la. The mind must see more than the camera. Or maybe there is a link or something when you are looking at each other at the instant..."

He stopped speaking and his face froze in shock. "Oh, my God!" he exclaimed. "This is my fault. I shouldn't be here. When I saw him, he saw me. He must have found out my name."

Turning to David he said excitedly, "That's what you said you need, isn't it... a face and a name? Then you can come to anyone, anywhere in the world."

"He didn't need your true name," David said softly. "He could know you as 'the lieutenant who saw me.' That would be a unique enough identifier for someone as skilled as he is. With that, he could go into the mirror looking for you."

"And now he has seen you and Chi," General Crossford said.

"Hopefully," David replied, "he thinks we're dead. ... We should be. I don't know who trained him, but he knows about the Place of Chaos and Fire. At least he knows that nobody comes back from outside the bubble. He saw Chi fall through the boundary. He kicked me and I was falling toward the boundary when I chose to go into the darkness. He may figure I went through like Chi and both of us are dead."

"And if he comes back?" Mark asked.

"This place has to look like Chi and I are dead," David said flatly. "It has to be closed down."

"And where will you go?" Mark asked almost angrily. "At least your bodies– your flesh selves, or whatever you want to call it– they will be safe here."

"No!" David answered loudly. His voice took on an obvious edge of anger as he continued, "Chi and I will go someplace safe. And then we are going to track this man down and stop him!"

"He could be anywhere," Robert said, "and you don't know his name."

"I have seen his face," David replied. "And I know his name. His name is 'The Intruder.'"

"But you're no match for him," Mark said. "Trying to go up against him hand to hand again is suicidal and you know it. It will just get you and Chi killed."

He pointed to the monitor and said emphatically, "We have a face. Maybe we can find him on this side of the mirror."

"Looks Russian," the general said, leaning in to look more closely at the monitor.

"Possibly of the Volga Tatars," said David, "Far eastern Russia or northern China."

He then shrugged his shoulders and said, "I did a paper on them in college for an anthropology class. The combination of Eurasian features and Asian eyes is somewhat distinctive. But just because he traces his heritage back to there doesn't mean he's working for the Russians or the Chinese or anyone else."

"I think he's freelance," Mark said slowly. "If he was working for a given country, he wouldn't be trying to sell secrets on the open market."

"That gets you dead," Robert added with a tight smile.

"So how do we find a mercenary spy who could be anywhere in the world?" General Crossford said.

"To catch a thief..." David said slowly.

"Noooooooooo..." Robert said, raising his hands up in front of himself. "Ain't no way in..."

"He is theoretically on our side now," Mark interrupted, cocking his head slightly as if he were trying to convince himself this was a good idea.

"Who is this theoretical ally?" General Crossford asked.

"Frank Lufton," David, Mark, and Robert said in unison.

"Frank Lufton!" the general gasped. "Frank Lufton, the mercenary?!" she sputtered. "He has the morals of an alley cat. He would sell his grandmother to the highest bidder." She was shaking her head from side to side. "We could never trust him with something like this."

"He's already met me," David said with a smile. "And he knows I'm a mirror-walker."

"And Chi," Robert said.

"In fact," David continued, "we're almost friends. I was his guest at the beach for a couple of months."

"He already knows about the mirror-walkers," the general said slowly, "and he hasn't tried to sell that information?"

"Let's just say," Mark said, "that he now has an exclusive contract with the United States government. Specifically the President."

"Douglas Travis," Robert said, "made him an offer he couldn't refuse."

"Last I heard," the general replied, "he was working exclusively for Everett Connors."

"Yeah," Robert continued, "that didn't work out so good for either of them."

"I know enough not to ask," General Crossford said tersely, "but I have to. Did you bring down Everett Connors?"

"He brought himself down," David said bitterly, "when he decided to try to overthrow the government and start World War Three." He paused and added much more softly, "I just got in his way."

David took a deep breath and then said, "In any case, I hold no ill feelings against Frank Lufton. He is an ethical mercenary, if such a thing exists. His men treated me OK and he was not responsible for either attempt on Chi and Momma Ling, nor the collateral damage from both. In fact he was very upset that people died unnecessarily. He has given his word that he has an exclusive contract with the US, and he will keep that word."

Mark spoke up. "And most importantly," he said, "he is probably the only cleared source we can go to who has any chance of finding our rogue mirror-walker

90

in the flesh."

"I will arrange for General Johansson to visit him," General Crossford said.

"I don't think that's a good idea," Mark said slowly.

When the general gave him a quizzical look, he continued, "I don't think Frank wants that much brass walking in his front door unannounced. He might not be as willing to do this as if say, David and I paid him a little visit."

"And me," Robert chimed in. "I think he actually liked me," he added with a smile.

"You might be right," the general said. "But we need to coordinate this with Washington. In any case, I will arrange to have a bird here at first light and you can be in New Orleans by mid-afternoon."

***

The "bird" was a Marine Chinook C-47F painted in tan desert camo. And it was already sitting on the ground with its engines warmed and ready when the sun finally cast a glow over the horizon. The general walked with Mark, Robert, David, and a squad of Marine guards over to the waiting helicopter. The Marines formed a defensive perimeter around the helicopter while the three men and the general went to the open side door of the Chinook.

"Isn't this a little bit of overkill?" Robert said as they stood next to the helicopter. "There're only three of us. You could carry a whole platoon in this thing."

"And all their gear," the general replied. "But it's the fastest bird in the air and has enough range to go to New Orleans and back from here." She looked around the parking lot. "Besides," she continued, "the locals are used to these birds coming in and out ferrying supplies. And there's room to land it on the Connors building."

"I'm surprised Lufton's still in the same place," Robert said.

"You forget, big brother," Mark said, "that the government seized a lot of Connors' assets... including a very, very secure building in downtown New Orleans."

"How long will it take?" David asked.

"The flight?" replied the general. "Or convincing Lufton to do this?"

"The flight," David said flatly.

"With this light a load," General Crossford replied, "the 47F can reach nearly two hundred miles per hour... more if the wind is with you. You should sitting on top of the Connors Building in about seven hours."

"Chi is supposed to join us," David said, "and I don't want her to be in the mirror any longer than she has to."

"Want her to save her strength?" Robert said kiddingly.

"No," David replied almost harshly, "I don't want The Intruder to find her in the mirror alone. He's nearly gotten her twice. We can't assume we're safe because he thinks we might be dead. He's a professional. He will verify his kills."

"David," Robert said slowly, "you're starting to scare me."

David looked at him and frowned. "The Intruder," he said harshly, "is a very cold-blooded killer who must be stopped. And Chi and I may be the only ones who can stop him."

"Don't forget Frank Lufton," Mark said quickly. "He's captured mirror-walkers before– namely you. He knows how to do it and how to handle them once he's got them."

"I don't think you're going to find The Intruder standing in front of a mirror in an unguarded bedroom." David replied.

He started to say something else, but the crew chief on the Chinook shouted down, "All aboard. Let's get this bird in the air."

Chapter Fourteen
A Necessary Frenemy

The flight was almost exactly seven hours long. Around noon, the crew chief offered his passengers a choice of MREs or a small pack of cookies and a chocolate bar. Robert and the crew chose the MREs. Mark and David settled for the cookies and chocolate bar.

"You know, these Meals Ready to Eat really aren't all that bad," Robert said as he added some water from a bottle into the bag. "You should try them."

Mark turned to David and said, "They are probably better than anything he fixes for himself, but I don't eat his cooking either."

As the afternoon wore on, David was beginning to regret not eating something more substantial. His stomach was upset and rumbling by the time the Chinook set down on the Connors Building heliport a little after 2:30 local time.

The guard on the roof door waved them through without checking their identification, but a second security point just inside demanded full identification. "Will this do?" Mark said softly as he showed his Secret Service credentials. Robert showed his police badge and ID from Plain City. David pulled out his driver's license and said softly, "I'm with them."

"No," Mark said very firmly. "We are with him, and he is expected on the ninth floor."

"Oh," the guard said, checking his clipboard. "Yes... a Mister David Malone... and escorts. You are cleared for the ninth floor. Please proceed to the elevator."

"You will need this," he said as he started to hand Mark a special elevator key.

"No, I won't," Mark answered as he held up an identical key. "Like I said, we're expected."

David didn't hear what the guard was mumbling as they walked past him and into the elevator.

"Good to know security is good here," Robert said.

"Security is bullshit here," Mark retorted almost angrily. "I took this key off the board behind him while he was checking his clipboard."

David just laughed and said to Robert, "And I'm starting to scare you?"

Mark looked at him angrily and would have said something, but the elevator doors opened at that point.

The blonde receptionist guard wasn't holding her hand under her desk as they stepped out of the elevator like she had the last time David was here. Instead, her hand was on a large, semi-circular pad that somewhat resembled a game controller. Her eyes widened slightly as she recognized David.

"We come in peace," David said with a smile. "And we're expected," he added firmly.

Without raising her hand from the pad, the receptionist looked down quickly at a piece of paper on her desktop. She then relaxed and brought her hands together in front of her.

"Nice upgrade of the weaponry," Robert said. "I assume the pad controls multiple weapons." He then pointed at what appeared to be five security cameras above her desk. They were all currently pointed at the open elevator doors.

"Ultra-High-Velocity projectiles," she answered calmly. "Only one-seven-seven caliber, but almost two inches long. I think they call them needle rounds. The mechanism is gas-driven and can deliver up to one hundred rounds a minute if I keep my finger on the button."

"A little indiscriminate don't you think?" Mark said

firmly. "There'd be collateral damage if everyone wasn't an unfriendly."

"Facial recognition targeting," she replied with a smile. "Locked on to you from the cameras in the elevator. All I have to do is select an image and press the button. Or, if things are really going south, I can just hit the knee switch and the button at the same time."

"Knee switch?" David asked.

"It means full incursion," she replied. The smile left her face. "Anything that isn't me in this room is targeted automatically and the guns don't stop 'til they're empty."

"Dangerous times," Robert said shaking his head. "Dangerous times."

"We were told to expect four of you," the blonde said flatly.

David looked at her and raised his eyebrows.

"Oh," she said, trying to smile. "Your Chinese friend. I assume she is here, but isn't here."

"Yeah," David said, "and we really need to speak with Mister Lufton."

"I will buzz you in," she replied.

"No need," David answered as he started to move past the desk. "You've changed to a double offset. Currently it's forty-five seconds fast followed by eighty-two seconds slow." He looked back at her with a big smile and said, "And it changes four times a day."

She shook her head and then motioned toward the door with her hand and said, "He's expecting you."

David keyed the proper numbers into the security lock and the door to Frank Lufton's office buzzed open. An older woman was seated at a desk facing the door. She was typing on a keyboard and did not bother to lift her head from her work. "You know the way," she said brusquely.

"Thank you," David said quickly as they walked

past her into the inner office.

"Mister Malone," Frank said, rising from the seat behind his desk. "... and the Nash brothers. What brings you to my office on this fine afternoon?"

"I assume the President briefed you on what is happening." Mark said.

"He told me only that you were coming," Frank replied calmly, as he returned to his chair. "And that I should believe whatever you told me and act on it as if it were coming directly from him."

"We have a rogue mirror-walker," David said firmly as he slid the picture of The Intruder onto the desk.

"You've got his picture?" Frank said in surprise.

"And we have a way to detect a mirror-walker in a room," Mark answered.

He paused and then added, "As long as there aren't too many people already in the room and the walker comes in where we expect him and has the properties we expect."

"So how can we be sure that we are alone right now?" Frank asked.

David held up his phone. The text said, "Clear."

"Chi?" Frank asked.

"Chi," David answered.

"So," Frank said slowly, "what can I do for you?"

"There is someone in the mercenary community... your community... who has information for sale," Mark began. "It is information that no one could possibly have obtained legally or any other way and, as such, is extremely valuable. We need you to figure out who they are, track them down, and neutralize them. If possible, the rogue is to be brought back as a captive, but other solutions are acceptable if absolutely necessary."

He paused and said, "We really want this rogue in custody so we can find out more about him. The rest of his operation is expendable... if necessary."

Frank stared silently at the three men for several minutes. Finally he took a deep breath and spoke. "This is more than a black op," he said slowly, obviously choosing his words very carefully. "This is wet... possibly very wet," he added tensing up his mouth and his entire face.

After another long pause he sighed. "Times have changed, Mister Nash," he said sadly. "This country doesn't approve of such things anymore. I could end up testifying before Congress... and then on trial... and then possibly going to prison if the administration changes.

"Did the President give you a code name for this operation?" Mark asked calmly.

"Yes," Frank replied. "He called it Project Intruder."

Mark slid a single page onto Frank's desk. The letterhead bore the Presidential seal. Beneath the ornate letterhead was a single, long, printed sentence: "Because this action is vital to the defense and security of our nation, Frank Lufton and Connors Security, or its subsidiaries, is hereby authorized to complete Project Intruder fully and completely by any means necessary." Beneath that line was the President's signature followed by seven military signatures.

"That's your *Get out of Jail Free* card," Robert said as Frank picked up the paper.

"Signed by the President and all members of the Joint Chiefs," Mark said. "That gives you full authorization for a military action."

"Or an assassination," Frank added softly. "I know the routine."

He pursed his lips for a moment and then said "The rogue mirror-walker is the key to all of it. If we take him down, it falls apart."

"Easier said than done," David said, almost angrily.

"I underestimated you," Frank replied quickly, "or at least Mister Connors did. I'm not underestimating what this rogue can do."

He locked eyes with David and said, "Why can't you and your Chinese friend just take care of this in the mirror?"

"No weapons in the mirror," David answered, "...just your own body. He's big, well-trained, and ruthless. We think he's possibly killed other mirror-walkers. We hope he thinks he killed Chi and me."

He paused and then said more softly, "Or next time he might succeed."

"So I have to catch him outside the mirror," Frank said evenly, "before he catches you or Chi in the mirror."

"Bingo!" Robert said loudly, drawing stern looks from Frank, Mark, and David.

"Crude, but correct," Frank said with a smile. He exhaled deeply and then said, "I'll see what I can do. How do I report? How do we share information?"

"A General Crossford or General Johansson will be contacting you with further logistical information," Mark answered. "Anything we find out will come to you through them."

"How did you get old Triple J on board with this?" Frank asked. He was obviously surprised.

"I can be very convincing," David said with a smile.

Frank laughed loudly. "That you can," he said as he continued to laugh. "I learned that the hard way."

He looked at the three of them and asked, "Is there anything else I need to know? Or maybe something I can do for you right now?"

David and Mark shook their heads, but Robert suddenly smiled and said, "As a matter of fact, Mister Lufton, there is."

***

About a half hour later, Mark, Robert, and David walked back out to the heliport on the top of the Connors Building. Robert was smiling broadly and carrying a tall stack of pizza boxes from Vieux Carre Pizza.

As he handed the boxes to a waiting crewman, he said, "I think I brought enough for everyone. And there should be something you like... unless one of you is a pure Vegan who won't eat cheese– or worse, someone who wants pineapple and sauerkraut on a ham pizza."

"Who would do that?" one of the crewmen said in disgust.

"You've never been to Iowa," Mark answered. "And you've never met Happy Joe or his pizzas."

"We brought Coke, Pepsi, Sprite, Mountain Dew, and Root Beer," David said. "I hope that works. It's what we have at family gatherings and seems to work for us."

"In Iowa?" the crewman asked with a laugh.

"Not everything in Iowa is weird!" Robert said in mock anger. "It's just... ... ... different."

The crewman laughed again and said, "My momma told me to always time the blank space before the word different. The longer the space the more 'different' it is. Looks like Iowa is a seven-second different."

"What about this operation?" David asked calmly.

"Well," the crewman answered, "it's... ... ... different."

"You got that right," Robert answered with an umph as the Chinook rose rapidly into the air in what felt like a corkscrew spiral.

"What about the pilots?" David asked.

"They're OK," the crewman answered. "They just

100

had a bad feeling about this whole thing and decided to take off using maximum avoidance.

"I meant, can they take time to eat?" David said. "But I would like to ask them if the tight spin was really necessary."

"The tight spin was to help prevent a heat lock-on from a shoulder-fired." the crewman said.

He chuckled and said, "Never show your tailpipe to someone long enough for them to get a bead on it."

"That's good advice," Robert said with a smile. Then he added, "... in many situations."

"And as far as eating," the crewman continued, "there are three pilots on board. One of them can sit back here with us and eat while the other two fly this thing."

A crewman whom David had not seen before reached in to grab a slice of pizza. A higher-pitched voice said, "The co-pilot can also eat in position as long as she or he is ready to take over control if they have to."

David looked up at the woman who had spoken. There were pilot's wings on the front of her uniform.

"But never eat anything at the controls that you aren't willing to wear," she said with a smile. Then she cocked her head slightly and said, "I dropped a full chocolate milkshake onto my lap once when a bird strike came through the pilot's window and I had to suddenly take over the controls."

Robert muttered softly, but loud enough to be heard, "I'd have dropped a full load of chocolate somewhere else."

Mark looked at him and scowled, but the crew, including the pilot, laughed loudly.

***

Evidently the co-pilot wasn't willing to wear pizza,

because she waited for the reserve pilot to relieve her before coming back. After she ate and returned to the cockpit, the last pilot came back for his supper.

"I didn't know if it was appropriate to ask," David said slowly, "and I didn't want to insult anyone, but are there a lot of female pilots in the Marines?"

"There are a lot of female Marines in the Marines," the pilot answered firmly. "Never underestimate someone just because they are a woman," he added harshly.

"You've gotta meet Momma Ling," Robert said. "You would know that no one here ever underestimates a woman."

"Sounds like a woman I would like to meet," the pilot said with a smile.

"Who knows?" Robert answered. "Maybe she or her granddaughter will fly with us sometime."

"Or maybe she is already here," the pilot said softly.

When David and the Nash brothers looked at him with wide-eyed, startled expressions, he smiled slightly and continued, "Mister Malone, we know you are a mirror-walker, and we know what that is. We also know about Kong Ling and her granddaughter. We were part of the operation after you rescued the First Lady. We didn't go in, and we weren't told everything, but we were part of the perimeter defense and could hear the radio chatter. That's why this bird– and this crew– for your trip to New Orleans."

His voice became very firm as he said, "I also know what you've done for your country, Mister Malone, and it's an honor to have you aboard. We might very well meet again."

As he walked back toward the cockpit carrying a piece of pizza, he called back, "Oh, and thank you for the pizza. This is what I call a meal ready to eat."

Robert chuckled and said, "You know, I like that guy."

Chapter Fifteen
A Second Intrusion

It was a little after midnight when they got back to the mine at Copper Harbor. A light snow was starting to blow, but visibility was still within limits for them to land. General Crossford was there to meet them when the bird set down in the parking lot. So was Chi, and of course, Kong Ling.

"We have to enter the mine through the emergency exit," the general said softly. "It isn't safe to come in the front way."

"Problem with the mine?" Robert asked cautiously.

"Testing some new defense measures," the general replied tersely. The she added, "Let's get below."

A few minutes later they were winding down a very tall– and very shaky– spiral staircase that seemed to go straight down into the heart of the mine. At several points doors opened into the tourist areas.

"Are you sure this will hold all of us?" Robert asked when they were about halfway down.

General Crossford laughed, "It is designed to hold four full tour groups in case they have to evacuate due to a sudden water incursion or a geological shift."

Mark laughed and said, "That means in case of flood or earthquake, big brother."

"I knew what it meant," Robert said indignantly. "I was just trying not to think of it."

David spoke up, "The flood danger would probably only be during the spring melt off and this area is geologically very stable."

"Yeah," answered Robert, "and everything else going on around us is obeying the ordinary laws of nature."

His comment evidently gave everyone something to

think about, because they all remained silent as they tromped the rest of the way down to the lowest areas of the mine. At the base of the stairs was a heavy hatch which normally sealed the escape route. Two guards stood ready on either side of the opening.

"Looks like a submarine hatch," David observed.

"Probably installed by the Navy," Robert replied as he pulled it closed behind them so the other door to the mantrap would be able to open.

Once they were back in the living quarters, Mark asked, "What are these defensive measures you are testing?"

"Let's just say," the general answered, "that you absolutely do not want to walk up to the front entry area without clearing it with security in advance."

She paused and said, "I'll show you part of it." Then she signaled them to follow her and began walking up one of the long corridors.

When she reached the outer security door, she turned and said, "Do NOT step through this door." She then cautiously opened it to reveal the back of a strange-looking gun with nine barrels. A string of strange-looking nails held together by two thin plastic ribbons trailed down from the barrels to a large ammunition-style case sitting beneath it. Thick tubing ran from the back of the gun to a large pipe that had been laid on the floor.

"This," she explained, "is one of Connors Armaments latest developments. "It uses highly compressed air to fire a .177 needle round."

"Up to one hundred rounds per minute," Mark added. "And it can be camera and facial-recognition controlled."

"Correct," said the general, somewhat surprised that Mark knew that information. "But in this case they are triggered by Lieutenant Anderson's detection arrays.

Anything shows positive as a mirror-walker and this gun sprays the area."

"Isn't that a little dangerous for, you know, the rest of us humans down here?" Robert asked.

"It's a trap," Mark said firmly. "They're risking it because they think the rogue will come back."

"I would," said David. "He has to know that we somehow detected him and will come back to see how we did it."

"Mister Malone," General Crossford began, "if it were you, would you home in on a person or the room to come back?"

"The room," David answered. "The person might have moved and what I would want to see is the room and how they detected me."

"That's what we are thinking," the general explained. "Right now the outer rooms are empty except for thirty-seven of these air Gatlings."

"Why thirty-seven?" Robert asked.

"That's all they had available for immediate shipment," the general answered. "But we've got pretty good coverage of all forward areas with overlap in the old security room."

The general turned again to David and asked, "If you were going to break in here, when would you do it?"

"Normally, it wouldn't really matter," he answered after a short pause, "but if I thought they had a way of detecting me, I would probably wait until the middle of the night."

"Meaning?" asked the general.

"Somewhere near one am," David answered. "By then, the night shift will have checked everything over and be settling into their standard boring routine."

"If we're right," the general said firmly, "tonight will be anything but boring."

As if to confirm her words, the gun in front of them

suddenly sprang to life with an ear-splitting roar. From the cacophony sounding from other nearby places it was obvious that more than one of the weapons had activated.

After what seemed like twenty or thirty minutes, but was in reality ninety seconds, the guns went silent. They were out of ammunition.

"Positive identification of intruder," a voice over the internal speakers said.

"We need you or Chi to check to see if he is still here," the general said softly. Then she added, "We will deactivate the remaining weapons."

"That will be me," David said as he turned and walked toward his mirror room. Robert quickly followed him.

"Come to the conference room afterwards," the general yelled to him as he walked up the hallway.

A few minutes later, the group was gathered in the conference room. David entered wearing his robe.

"The area is clean," he said flatly. "Or at least I didn't see the mirror-walker. Everything has been reduced to rubble, however. Any human in there would have been cut to shreds."

"Are you saying the rogue isn't human?" Mark asked.

"No," David replied, "I'm saying those weapons would be very indiscriminate in who they kill."

"Do you think it killed him?" the general asked.

"Yes and no," David answered. "It possibly killed– if you can call it that– his mirror self. We have no way of knowing. Perhaps it did. But you killed me by turning off the lights... and being sucked out of a jet possibly killed Chi, but all that happened was that we returned to our flesh selves."

He looked over at Chi who was trembling slightly at his talk of dying in the mirror and continued, "As we found out, the only way to truly kill– or injure– a mirror-walker is to do it in the Place of Fire."

"Or," Mark added, "to kill the flesh body."

At that point, Harold entered the room. "Well, Lieutenant," the general said, "did we get him?"

"He went down," the lieutenant answered. "Here," he said pointing a remote at a monitor on the wall. "You can see what the scanners recorded."

A very smeary, blue-green image appeared on the monitor. It wasn't very clear, but it was obviously the rogue mirror-walker.

"This is high-speed footage," Harold said, "so the playback is in slow motion. I will speed it up."

He pointed the remote at the monitor once again and the smeary figure began running toward the screen.

"Evidently," Harold continued, "he knows that there is some sort of detection system in the first room, so he was running toward the hallway to get through the room as fast as possible. Maybe he was hoping that we would think it was a false detection."

"Maybe they have already developed detectors of some sort," David said, "but haven't figured out how to rule out the large number of false positives like we have."

"We still have some false positives," Harold said. "That's why the guns still have to be triggered manually by a human."

He shrugged his shoulders and said, "When the duty guard saw that the figure was running toward the living areas, he triggered all guns. It's really a mess down there."

The view on the screen changed. "This is the second gun," Harold said. "He ran right into this one."

The figure suddenly stood straight upright. Despite the blurriness, you could see the look of surprise– and pain– on the figure's face as he collapsed on the floor in

108

front of the gun.

"You killed him," the general said flatly.

"Only temporarily," David said. "He will feel like hell, but his flesh self is alive and his mirror self can come right back here again."

"Would you?" Harold asked.

"No," David said firmly, "not right back. I would take time to evaluate what had happened. He's probably worried that the next time we might actually kill him. I don't think he's had his mirror self killed before. He knows he has to use the Place of Fire to kill another mirror-walker, but I don't think anyone has ever actually defeated him in any way in the mirror."

"So what do we do?" the general asked. "What is our next step?"

"How many of these detectors do you have?" David asked Harold.

"As many as we need," the lieutenant answered. "They are a pretty stock item. We are just using them in an unusual way."

"Then I would say that Chi and I... and the team... stay here," David continued. "But we need these detectors everywhere and we need twenty-four seven computer monitoring of them against live feeds so we know immediately if we have company."

He turned to Chi and said, "I'm sorry, Chi, but they are going to have to reactivate the live cameras in our mirror rooms."

Momma Ling translated and Chi nodded her head

She says, "I understand," Momma Ling said softly. Then her voice turned harsh and she added, "But I do NOT!"

"If he comes looking for us," David said, turning to Kong Ling, "he will probably come through our mirrors. If he knows we are alive, he would know that whatever the counter-measures are, they are too destructive to be pointed at our mirrors."

"But he thinks you're dead," Robert added.

"We can only hope so," General Crossford said slowly.

"But he doesn't know that we are the only mirror-walkers you have," David said. "If he can, he will try to come in through our mirrors assuming that the defenses are weakest there whether we are alive or not."

"Well," Mark said, "I don't think there is anything else we can do tonight. David and Chi, you have had a long day. Get some sleep. We will meet again at thirteen hundred hours tomorrow."

"Are the weapons reset?" the general asked.

"We are waiting for the pressure in the lines to bleed off totally before entering the area," the lieutenant answered. "With all the guns firing, some of the controls were damaged and we don't know if they are all safe."

"How long?" the general asked.

Harold looked at his watch and said, "They should be entering the kill zone within the next fifteen minutes. Assuming that the damaged controllers can be quickly replaced, the defense wall should be back up in another half hour."

"Do you think he'll try again?" the general asked, looking at David.

"Not tonight," David answered. "If it were me, I would be drinking a couple of cups of hot chocolate to calm down and trying to understand what had happened."

"He's not from Iowa," Robert said. "He'll be drinking Scotch."

"Or Vodka," Mark added.

"Whatever," the general said harshly. "I will see you all at thirteen hundred hours tomorrow."

Chapter Sixteen
And Then There Were Three

David literally stumbled to his bedroom and fell face first onto his bed without taking off his clothes. He was exhausted and planned to sleep until at least noon. He was not happy, therefore, when Lieutenant Anderson tapped on his door a little after seven.

"Harold, is this really necessary?" he asked testily as he opened the door and saw who was there.

The lieutenant said nothing, but pointed into the room. David sighed and said "OK" as he opened his door. As they entered, Robert opened the door from the adjoining bedroom.

"Is everything all right?" he asked cautiously.

"No," Harold answered, "but I think I need to talk to David in private."

"I'd rather Robert was here," David answered. "And not because the general says it has to be that way. I'm so tired my brain is fried and Detective Nash has a way of cutting right to the heart of the matter."

Harold looked quickly between the two men and said, "If it has to be that way, OK. But this has to stay between just the three of us for now."

David sat on his bed and motioned for Harold to sit on the chair across from his desk. Robert stepped back through the door and grabbed a chair from his room.

The lieutenant sat staring at them for a moment and then said, "You may have noticed that I have been in and out of here a lot lately by helicopter."

"Actually," David said, "we hadn't noticed. We've been a bit busy ourselves."

"I'm sorry," Harold responded, "I guess you just assume everyone else notices what you are doing."

"That's OK," David said. "Just tell us what is going

on."

"I've been working with the Army trying to find more mirror-walkers," he said quickly.

"How in the hell are they doing that!?" Robert spurted out.

"Good question," David said. "How are they doing it?"

"I helped them come up with a system," the lieutenant said. "They bring whole platoons of soldiers into a large hangar. There are small dressing rooms created by tent barriers like they would use in massive casualty hospitals. Each dressing room has a mirror in it."

"Let me guess," Robert said angrily, "they are told to strip down and stare in the mirror and then report if they go anywhere." His voice became louder as he almost yelled out, "What are they trying to do, make these kids into fire fodder for that damned place of darkness!?"

"Again," David said– much more calmly– "Robert has expressed my concerns."

"These soldiers are practically imprinted on their sergeants," Harold said quickly. "They were told to look into their own eyes in the mirror and think about their sergeants. They were even told to keep repeating the sergeant's name while they stared in the mirror."

He looked over a Robert and said, "I knew about the Place of Fire or whatever you call it. I also knew that if you concentrated on a particular person you wouldn't go there."

"But something went wrong," David said softly.

"Yes... and no," Harold said, bobbing his head as he spoke. "We had all of the sergeants gathered together in a big curtained-off room with a large mirror set up at the front. Facing the mirror was a big whiteboard that said, "If you can read this, go back and report to Major

Gretz."

"I'm sorry I blew up on you," Robert said. "That sounds like a pretty good plan."

The lieutenant continued, "I had a ring of scanners set up pointing out around the outside of the room where the sergeants were. ... in case you know who showed up."

His voice crept slightly upward in pitch as he added, "I also had a couple of the full scanners set up to paint an image of whoever came directly into the room."

"And someone came into the room," David said flatly, "but didn't report to Major Gretz."

"Not exactly," Harold said. "He stuck his head through the door and stood there looking into the room. He must have come out of a mirrored surface inside the ring of scanners near the MPs who were guarding the doors. I think he's walked in mirrors before and didn't want anyone to know for some reason. Maybe he homed in on one of the guards or something."

"Why didn't you tell Major Gretz?" David asked softly.

"This guy looked scared– really scared," Harold answered, "like he was afraid that someone would find out about him."

Looking down at the floor, he continued, "I should have reported it to Major Gretz, but this man is a fellow mirror-walker to you... and I felt like I would somehow be betraying you if I turned him in."

"Then you know who he is?" Robert asked.

"Yes," Harold answered. Then he went quiet.

"It's OK," David said. "I think I know what to do."

Lieutenant Harold T. Anderson took a deep breath and said slowly, "Captain Marcus Robinson."

"Do you mean they were putting Captains in the little booths?" Robert said loudly.

"No," Harold answered, "Captain Robinson is

Military Intelligence of some sort. He was observing the operation. He told one of the MPs guarding the booths that he wanted to see exactly what the men were experiencing. I couldn't find out more than that without drawing attention to him."

"Do you have his cellphone number?" David asked.

"I can get it," replied Harold. "Are you going to call him?"

"Something like that," David said slowly. "Get me that number, and I will take it from there."

"I'll go with Harold to get the number and then meet you at the mirror room," Robert said. He was uncharacteristically business-like. David started to say something and then stopped.

Robert saw his face and continued in a very calm voice, "I know this is some serious shit that you have to handle all by yourself, but I'll help you where I can. Like always, I've got your back." He then gave a half smile and added, "And I will explain everything to my little brother if things go south."

"I'd rather you explained things to Chi," David answered. "I don't feel right leaving her out of this, but after everything else that has happened... it could be a trap."

"Yeah," Robert answered, "it's not like we haven't had to deal with deep infiltration of our own government in the past."

"This feels different," David said, "but..."

"I'll meet you in the mirror room in a few moments," Robert said as he and Lieutenant Anderson walked toward the door.

* * *

It was only about ten minutes before Robert entered the mirror room. David was already pacing nervously

114

back and forth in his robe. He pulled a cellphone from his pocket as soon as Robert entered the room.

"This is tied into the security system," he said quickly, "so I can send and receive texts. I am going to send Captain Robinson an invitation he can't refuse."

Several minutes later, Captain Marcus Robinson heard a soft chime indicating that a text message had come into his cellphone. As usual, he glanced down see who it was from. He didn't recognize the name at first, but then he saw the whole name. It said, "David Malone, Mirror Walker."

When he opened the text, it said simply, "I know you walk in mirrors but don't understand what is happening. I can explain. Image attached. Concentrate on my face and name and meeting me at Chou's tomb. I will be waiting."

Marcus looked quickly around his office. Satisfied that he would have privacy, he locked the door to his area and closed the blinds. He then opened a small closet in the bookshelves behind his desk. There was a full-length mirror mounted on the inside of the door. He set his phone so he could see David's image and then started unbuttoning his shirt. As he was taking off his shirt he gave a short chuckle and said aloud very softly, "I wonder if this is how Clark Kent felt in the phone booth?"

As he stared at himself in the mirror he thought *"David Malone... Chou's tomb... David Malone... Chou's tomb..."* A few minutes later he found himself standing in a small mausoleum. The young man who had sent the text was standing next to one tomb which somehow looked different from the rest.

"Chou requested his tomb be sealed with polished stone rather than rough rock or terra cotta," David said slowly. "That marble is the mirror which allows you to be here."

115

He slowly rubbed the face of Chou's tomb. His fingers sank slightly into the glossy marble. "He is also the reason I am here," he continued, "and why I understand a little of how mirror-walking works."

"How did you know I could do this?" Marcus asked. His question held both a hint of fear and a hint of anger.

"Curiosity caught the cat," David replied. "You were seen when you were checking out the recruitment efforts."

"How?"

"It's too technical for me to explain," David answered, "and I don't understand it myself. But the electronic wizards have a way of detecting a mirror-walker and even painting a smeary image of them. You came out of a mirror behind the perimeter detectors, but they painted an image of you when you stuck your head through the door to see what was happening."

"Then why am I not in Major Gretz's office getting royally reamed?" Marcus asked tersely.

"Because the tech who painted you thought you didn't want to be discovered," David answered, "so he came to me instead."

They stood looking at each other for a while, then David said, "I have two questions. How did you first go into the mirror? And, what do you know about mirror-walking?"

"I was in high school," Marcus replied, looking down slightly as if embarrassed. "I had a heavy crush on this really hot girl. One morning, I was getting ready to take a shower and I looked into the mirror. I was... imagining... the two of us showering together when suddenly I was in her bedroom. She was still in bed and was lying there sleeping. She had these stuffed animals all over the place and there was one big one that looked like that elephant from Sesame Street. She had that one pulled tight to her and was all curled up around it."

He looked up at David. "I thought it was all an hallucination," he continued, "but that day I tried to sit down with her and her friends at lunch." He gave a huff of amusement remembering the events. "They were all waaaaaay out of my league," he said, "but I was seventeen and high on hormones, so I gave it a try. I tried to ask her out." He huffed again and continued, "She just laughed at me. I don't know why I said it, but I told her, 'I guess you would rather date Snuffleupagus.'

"She freaked out. She stood up and started screaming at me, 'What have you been doing, pervert? Peeking through my bedroom windows!?'

"I stood up and said, 'I'm sorry. My friend dared me to say that.'

"She screamed back at me, 'Then your friend is a pervert, too!'

"The whole cafeteria was staring at me, so I took my lunch tray to a table way over in the corner and pretended I was in the room alone."

He shrugged. "But after that I knew that it was real. I played with it a little and figured out that there was a limited area I could see when I went through the mirror. If I went to the edge of that area, I could peek into a blackness that seemed to go on forever. There was what looked like a fire glow in the distance, but I never went in there because there were these really weird-looking dogs that came over to the edge and stared at me whenever I peeked in."

"It's a good thing you never went into that darkness," David replied. "You would have never come back. That is the Place of Chaos and Fire. If the dogs or the Fire Warriors find you there they will force you into the pit of fire. When that happens, your mirror self dies– permanently– and your body dies shortly thereafter."

"Good to know," Marcus replied quickly. "Are the

two guys in the red masks and weird armor the Fire Warriors?"

"I usually see them as black, but if they are carrying really big scimitars, then yes, that's probably them."

"They stayed in the distance," Marcus said, "so I didn't see them real clear."

"Speaking of seeing things," David continued, "Have you ever used it for your spy work?"

Marcus laughed. "I'm not a spy," he answered. "At least not a field agent. One of the problems with being an African-American is that everyone in the world immediately recognizes you as an American."

He laughed again. "Did you know," he continued, "that most Africans consider me white... a white American? Makes it hard to be a spy and blend in with the local populace anywhere but in the US."

His voice returned to normal as he said, "I'm a translator. I have this gift for picking up languages easily. I mainly sit in my office all day translating sensitive intercepts in dialects that don't quite match the main-stream language of their country."

"I was hoping you were James Bond," David said. "That's what we really need at the moment."

"What's going on?" Marcus asked. "Can you read me in?"

"You're already in," David replied. "I will tell you what to say to Major Gretz so you can be fully briefed, but first let me give you a few details about mirror-walking. You are the fourth active mirror-walker that we are aware of. There is you, me, Chi– Chou is her grandfather– and The Intruder. The Intruder is a rogue mirror-walker who is stealing information and selling it to the highest bidder. He tried to kill Chi and me by forcing us into the Place of Fire."

David paused. His voice became very terse as he said slowly, "If he sees you, he will kill you."

"Understood," Marcus said, tensing up nervously.

"Just as important," David said firmly, "never go into nothing. You've been lucky so far, but don't do that. Always have a place or person in mind or you could end up with the dogs and Fire Warriors."

"Understood," Marcus said again. This time his answer seemed a little more firm.

"And we can only meet here– in the mirror," David added, "because The Intruder has seen my face and may home in on my flesh body. If you need to talk to me text 'Chou' or 'tomb' and maybe a time to my phone. I will meet you here as soon as possible."

"Can't he come here?" Marcus asked.

"He could," David replied, "but we are hoping that he thinks we are dead. And right now, he doesn't know about you."

"What do you need me to do?" Marcus asked.

David smiled. "This is the message you need to give to Major Gretz. Tell him that David Malone told you that Frank Lufton needs a liaison for Operation Intruder and that Mark Nash will handle the introductions. That will get things rolling from your end. I will get things started from my end."

"OK" Marcus said, "but I need to get back before someone starts worrying and unlocks my office door."

"One last thing," David said, "you can trust Frank Lufton at least 95% of the time."

"What about the other 5%?" Marcus asked.

"Just keep it in mind," David said as Marcus shimmered and disappeared.

***

Captain Marcus Robinson shook his head slightly as he turned away from the mirror. Someone was tapping on his office door. "Is everything alright in there?" a nervous voice asked.

"Just changing clothes," he replied.

"For fifteen minutes?" the voice asked. There was a touch of irritation in her voice.

"Got lost in thought," he replied. "I think I figured out an answer to a problem that's been bugging me for a long time."

Chapter Seventeen
Taking Command

David turned from the mirror and reached for his robe. He looked tired. More tired than he had looked the night before. As he turned to walk toward the door, Robert arched his eyebrows and asked, "Well?"

David looked over at the mirror and took a deep breath. Then he looked over at Robert and said, "I think it's time to wake up your little brother... and General Crossford... and Chi."

A few minutes later, Robert's voice came over the speaker system. "Sorry to disturb your morning," he said gleefully, "but this is an important announcement. The meeting in the conference room scheduled for one o'clock– I mean thirteen hundred hours– has been rescheduled for oh eight thirty. Someone make sure that General Crossford, Kong Ling, Chi, Mark Nash, Lieutenant Anderson and all the guards and techs are awake and ready."

He paused a moment and then said with even more glee in his voice, "See you in thirty-five minutes."

***

David and Robert were sitting in the conference room when Mark burst through the doors. "What in the heck is going on?!" he demanded loudly.

Robert just smiled at him. David looked at him and answered calmly, "There is another mirror-walker."

Mark stopped in the doorway and stood staring at his brother and David. His arms had dropped to his side. His face was blank. His mouth was slightly open, but he was saying nothing.

"On our side," Robert said. "He and David were

just talking."

"Who?" Mark said quickly. "Where?"

"The walls have ears," David replied. "So no names out loud. But he should be telling Major Gretz in a few minutes that you need him as a liaison for Operation Intruder. I told him you would give him a full briefing.

"Where is he stationed?" Mark asked.

David looked shocked and stared at Mark for several moments before suddenly bursting into laughter. "I don't know," he said, still laughing. "I really don't know," he continued. "I've only talked to him in the mirror. Lieutenant Anderson found him. He will have all that information."

"Your bird leaves in five minutes," the lieutenant said quickly. Neither David nor Mark had noticed when he entered the room.

"To where?" Mark asked. He was starting to sound irritated.

"Eyes only, need to know," Harold replied. "This has to be kept really close to the vest."

"I guess I don't need to know it," Robert said with a chuckle. "And the lieutenant here can't say it out loud anyway, so nobody is going to find out from me."

"Who knows?" Mark asked. He still sounded angry, but it looked like his anger was now more directed at his brother who continued to make light of the situation.

"Me," Harold replied, "the pilots on the bird, and Major Gretz. That's all for now. And the pilots only know where, not who."

The lieutenant looked around the room for a moment before saying very softly, "I'm not sure of the classification of this particular piece of information but I think you all need to know it." He turned to Mark and said, "After you brief this person, you will accompany him or her to Frank Lufton and... introduce them." He paused and then said, "After that they will be a part of

Mister Lufton's team."

General Crossford came into the room just in time to hear Harold's whispered words. Her response was almost immediate. Her anger was only partially concealed as she said tersely, "Who in the hell made this decision to put an untested mirror-walker in the hands of a questionable privateer?"

"I did," David said firmly.

The general turned to face him as he continued emphatically, "He... or she... needs someone to protect them as soon as it becomes known that there is another mirror-walker in this game. And they can't come here because we are already compromised."

He looked around the table and then back at the general before saying, "I know you don't trust Frank Lufton, General, but there are reasons which I cannot speak that make me very confident that this particular mirror-walker will not be corrupted by their involvement with a mercenary."

The general looked at David for a long time before replying, "Normally, I would object to this arrangement, but..." she let out an audible sigh before continuing, "I have to trust you as the head of the mirror-walkers."

David nodded and looked around the room. Was he the head of the mirror-walkers? He was uncomfortable with that, but it was evidently true.

"So," General Crossford continued, "From what I have learned, Special Agent Nash and Lieutenant Anderson need to leave immediately."

Turning to them she asked, "When will you return?"

"Round trip flight time is seventeen hours, Ma'am," Harold replied. "Less if the winds are with us, but there will be time on the ground at both stops."

"Then you'd better get going, Lieutenant," the general said brusquely, "while we figure out what to do in the meantime."

"Yes, Ma'am," Harold said as he shot to his feet. Mark rose a little more slowly and nodded to the general as he walked toward the door.

"Now," the general said, turning to face the group still sitting at the table, "what is the plan for today?"

"The technicians," David replied, "need to get the detection system up and running and they will need us in the mirror to test things... except the guns."

General Crossford nodded.

"But first," he continued, "I need to introduce Chi to the new mirror-walker."

Kong Jing nodded in agreement after her grandmother translated.

"Then we have no further business this morning... do we?" the general said.

When everyone around the table shook their heads, she added, "I do want to speak with you, David, in private for just a moment."

As everyone else filed out of the room, Robert looked over at him, and David said, "You can wait just outside the door. I think we can trust General Crossford."

Robert nodded his head and walked toward the door. "I don't trust anybody completely," he said as he closed the door and then opened it back up just a little.

"You will trust me!" the general said harshly and Robert again pulled the door closed.

When the door had latched with a loud click, the general said softly, "You know about the recruitment efforts." It was more of a statement than a question.

David nodded his head.

"And this person was one of the people tested?" she continued. This time it was slightly more of a question.

"Not exactly," David answered. "And I think your method is good, but could be better."

"What do you mean?" the general asked.

"Once this is all over," he said firmly, "they should be directed to a mirror-walker in the mirror who could speak with them and explain what's happening. Then there should be a special... basic training... for mirror-walkers so they don't get themselves killed."

"And so they don't abuse their powers," the general added firmly.

David wasn't sure that she wasn't hinting of his own actions so he said, "Yes, I am against the military use of mirror-walkers. And I think that mirror-walkers of all nations should be one cooperative body... perhaps under the supervision of the United Nations. Then mirror-walkers could be used for what we can do best, *FINDING PEOPLE*. We can move through rubble to find survivors in earthquakes, and we can move through fires to find people trapped in buildings or wildfires. We can be a great service to humanity."

He stopped. His shoulders were slumped as he said almost flatly, "Once this is all over and we get past having to stop bad guys."

"But there's always another bad guy," the general said. David noticed that her voice sounded almost as flat and devoid of emotion as his had been.

"Yes," David said, "there is always another bad guy."

"Just remember that we are both on the same side," she said firmly.

"I won't undercut you," David said equally firmly. He instantly regretted that a soft voice in the back of his mind added, "... unless I have to."

He remained seated as the general rose and left the room. Setting his phone on the table he texted Marcus, "Chou's tomb, 15 minutes?"

A moment later a reply appeared on the screen, "K"

He sent a second text, this one to Chi who also had

a special phone. Then he walked slowly down the hallway to his mirror room. Robert, as always, walked close behind him watching for any possible danger. The two armed Marines trailed behind them.

Marcus was at the tomb when David arrived. "Why can't I read it?" he asked, pointing at the Chinese writing on the face of the tomb.

"Don't know," David answered, "but that's the way it works. Printed words don't translate, but spoken ones do, even if they are recorded." He laughed slightly and asked, "Have you tried watching foreign language TV while you're in the mirror?"

"No," Marcus answered, somewhat surprised. "Does that really work?"

"It does for me and Chi," David answered. "She can watch English films or whatever and I can watch Chinese."

His face relaxed and he smiled broadly, "We both watched a Russian documentary and neither of us can speak Russian."

"Interesting," Marcus said, obviously considering the new knowledge.

A soft, feminine voice suddenly asked, "Can he move the barriers?" It then added, "He may need that if he meets The Intruder."

"Oh," David said, "you startled me. I didn't know you had arrived."

Turning to Marcus he said, "Captain Marcus Robinson, this is Kong Jing from Penglai, Shandong, China. Most of us call her Chi, which is the way the mirror translates her name for me."

Marcus looked embarrassed and flustered.

"You will get used to the lack of clothing," Chi said brightly. "And you can call me Kong Jing or Chi."

"I'm sorry, Jing," Marcus said. "I've gotten used to being naked with a bunch of soldiers for this or that, but

126

I guess I didn't expect a female."

"Expect anything," Chi responded firmly, "... and everything."

She turned to face David and said, "Back to my question, can he move the barriers?"

"I don't know what you mean, Jing," Marcus replied.

"This," David said and he raised his arms in a V above his head. "In!," he said loudly as he pulled his hands closer together."

Suddenly the barriers were right around them. Darkness could be seen at the edges of the now very small mirror bubble. The glow of the fires of chaos reflected off the face of Chou's tomb and the faces of the dogs of chaos could be see through the mist.

"And this... Out!," David said loudly as he moved his hands as far out from his body as he could. The mirror bubble returned to normal, or perhaps even well beyond normal.

"Shee-it!" Marcus exclaimed. "I didn't know it could do that!"

"The rogue can do it with just his thoughts," Chi said very firmly. "And if he catches you by surprise, you will end up in the Place of Chaos."

"You need to practice moving the barrier," David said calmly. "I hope it never comes to this, but you may need to be able to move the barrier back out to save yourself if The Intruder attacks you." He sounded like a teacher lecturing to a class, and he knew it, but that was what he was at this moment, a teacher.

"I wish I had time to teach you all that I know about the mirror," David said, "but we don't have time and each minute that I am with you increases the risk that The Intruder will learn of you."

"What about Frank Lufton?" Marcus asked. "You warned me about him."

"Frank Lufton," David said quietly, "is loyal to the person with the most power or the most money or both."

He paused to look at the wall between Chi and Marcus.

"Right now," he continued, "that is the President of the United States, but..."

"I will keep that in mind," Marcus said.

"One more thing," David said. He then turned to Chi and said something very quietly. A moment later Chi shimmered and disappeared.

"That's what it looks like when a mirror-walker leaves the mirror or goes somewhere else," he said. "If you see that, then someone– a mirror-walker someone– saw you and left. You will also look like that when you leave and it identifies you as a mirror-walker. If you see The Intruder, duck behind something before you leave or he will know you were there."

"What if he's already seen me?" Marcus asked. "Isn't it kind of obvious I'm walking around naked when everyone else has clothing?"

"If you see him and he has seen you, get out of the mirror immediately," David said. The volume and strength of his voice surprised him. "He can– and will– kill you in the mirror, but he can't touch you once you are back in the flesh world."

"But he can send his buddies to get me," Marcus said somewhat angrily.

"That's where you will have to trust Frank Lufton," David replied with a very tight smile. "He has buddies, too. And his buddies are on our side... I hope."

He paused for a moment and then said in a forced whisper, "You need to leave now. Our rogue mirror-walker could show up at any time." When Marcus appeared to have a question, David continued, "Besides, I need to talk to Chou."

"I thought he was dead," Marcus said, looking very

confused.

"It's complicated," David said with a short laugh. "And I didn't say anything about him talking back."

"I hope we can meet in person when this is all over," Marcus said, holding out his hand.

As David took his hand, he said, "We have met in person, just not in the flesh."

Marcus stepped back slightly. As he was shimmering away, David said softly, "Stay safe."

***

David stood staring a Chou's tomb for many minutes. Finally he said softly, "Am I really the head of the mirror-walkers?" His shoulders drooped as his arms dropped to his side. "Am I even capable of leading the mirror-walkers?" he said sadly. Then he added, "There is so much I don't know."

A quiet voice inside his head– perhaps his own thoughts, perhaps something more– said softly, "But you know that you do not know."

"Yes," David said with a sigh, "I know that I do not know."

He then shimmered and disappeared from the tomb.

"You look like hell," Robert said gruffly as soon as David turned from the mirror and picked up his robe.

"Short night," David said, shaking his head slightly and looking at his reflection in the mirror.

"While you were gone," Robert continued, "Momma Ling stuck her head in the door and said that Chi will handle the calibration tests this morning. Meanwhile, you can get some sleep and then work with the techs this afternoon."

"But one of us has to patrol," David said emphatically. "I can't leave her unprotected."

Robert gave David one of his irritating smiles and

pointed up. There were two strange-looking cameras mounted on the ceiling.

"Some of the techs didn't get a whole lot of sleep either," he said. "These cameras equipped with detectors are mounted all over the entire facility. If our rogue walker gets in, we will know."

He laughed slightly and added, "And he might get another taste of those needle guns."

"Isn't that playing a little loose with the lives of the rest of the people down here?" David asked, obviously concerned.

"The guns are set up in areas where they will be shooting at outside walls," Robert explained, "and it still takes an operator to trigger them." He pointed at the doorway and said, "Your guards have been re-stationed in the room across the hall so that the hallway is totally clear."

"I still think it's too dangerous," David said with a frown.

"Talk to General Crossford at tomorrow's briefing," Robert said. "But for now, you need some sleep."

When David didn't move Robert said ominously, "Don't make me sic Momma Ling on you."

David smiled and said, "OK, I'll get some sleep."

He grabbed his clothes, but then dropped them back over the chair on which they had been draped.

"I'll just wear the robe to my room," he said as he stepped out into the hallway. Robert, as usual, followed close behind.

Chapter Eighteen
Looking Through the Looking Glass

David startled and jumped to his feet looking wildly around his room for the source of what he thought was gunfire. He startled again as Robert once again rapped loudly on his door with something hard.

"You OK?" Robert's voice came through the door.

"Yeah," David called back. "I'm fine."

"I've been knocking and yelling for five minutes," Robert said. "If you didn't hear me using the coffee cup as a door knocker, I was coming in."

"I'll be right out," David said looking around the room for his clothes. After a moment, he remembered that he had worn his robe from the mirror room to his bedroom. He grabbed it and quickly wrapped it around his body.

"Door's open," he called out and Robert entered the room.

"You still look like hell," he said as he stood next to the open door.

"Thanks," David replied sarcastically, "but I actually feel better." Then he asked, "What time is it?"

"A little after two," Robert answered. "They only need you for a couple of tests," he said, "so it shouldn't be too hard."

He smiled and said, "You and Chi should maybe take the evening off together."

David glowered at him. "Or we could figure out how to trap The Intruder," he said almost angrily.

"Don't let your emotions take over," Robert said. His voice was uncharacteristically serious. "That will get you dead. You have to keep a clear head at all times if you are going to defeat this man."

"I know," David replied. His own voice was still

filled with anger, but his shoulders slumped slightly. His voice softened as he repeated, "I know." Then he said, "I'm just afraid that I won't get him before he gets Chi."

"We will figure out a way to catch him," Robert said firmly.

"We?" David asked.

"Someone has to think outside the box," Robert answered defensively.

"In your case," David replied, "you often think outside the warehouse."

"Whatever works," Robert replied as they walked out into the hallway. "Whatever works."

***

The technicians and security people indicated that they were ready for the tests, so David slipped out of his robe and stood in front of the mirror. He was just starting to feel the tug of the mirror when his face disappeared for a second from the mirror in front of him and he found himself staring into the eyes of the rogue mirror-walker.

He had never tried to stop himself from going into the mirror before. It felt as if he were being torn in two as he desperately tried to get back into his flesh body while still transitioning to the mirror. There was a confusing blur of light and images, but after a moment he was back out of the mirror.

"He's here!" he screamed as he turned from the mirror. "The Intruder just came through my mirror."

Robert was already speaking loudly into his intercom radio. "The Intruder is in the building," he almost yelled. "David is out of the mirror so anything that triggers is not him."

Almost as if in response to Robert's words, a short burst of air Gatlings exploded just outside the door in the hallway.

That was followed by an announcement over the speakers asking, "Does anyone have him on any of the detectors?"

There was a chorus of "No" through the radio after which General Crossford's voice commanded, "All weaponry to safety. Stations report status by the numbers."

"Station One, deactivated," a gruff voice answered.

"Station Two, deactivated," a female voice added.

After the count continued down through station twenty-three, the general's voice came back over the radio intercom. "David and Chi," she said, "would you please make a quick inspection of the area and then meet me in the conference room." There was a short pause and then she continued with, "Don't take any unnecessary chances."

"You heard her," Robert said, "don't take any unnecessary chances."

"If I can take him into the darkness with me," David said harshly, "I'll do it."

"There's got to be another way," Robert said, but David was no longer listening to him. He was staring intently at his own reflection in the black mirror. There was a deep intake of breath and Robert knew that David had gone into the mirror.

**

Twenty-five minutes later they were gathered in the conference room. Since Mark and Harold were with the new mirror-walker there were two empty seats. A staff sergeant technician was setting something up in the monitor as Robert and David entered the room. They were the last to arrive.

"Well, David," said General Crossford slowly,

133

"you've predicted exactly what this rogue was going to do up to now. What do you think is next?"

"That depends on what happened to him after he left my mirror room," David replied.

"I can answer that," the technician said quickly.

The general nodded and he started a short video on the monitor.

"This is high speed," he said, "so everything is in slow motion when it is played back."

David was intently studying the screen as the smeary green image of the dark-haired rogue pushed his way through the wall of the mirror room. The Intruder turned to run down the hallway, but an air Gatling at the end of the hallway opened up. The long, high-speed bullets appeared like long flashes of light in the video. They could be seen hitting the smeary image of the rogue directly in the chest. He turned toward the weapon with a look of rage on his face, then he disappeared."

"He knows now that you can't really kill him," David said flatly. "That means that all you did this time was really piss him off."

"But we drove him away," Robert said cheerfully.

"He'll be back," David said. His voice was starting to take on a touch of anger. "He knows I'm alive. I'm as much a threat to him as he is to me. He has to come back for me."

"What about Chi?" Kong Ling asked. "Do you think he saw her?"

"Doesn't matter," David said. "He will have to assume she is also alive until he has proof of her death." His voice became very hard as he said, "He'll be coming for her, too, now."

"I have a question about all this," Robert said, raising his hand like an old-fashioned orator trying to make a point. "How in the hell," he began, "did this guy know the exact moment that David was about to go into the mirror?"

He looked around the room before continuing, "And don't tell me it was a coincidence. The timing was too exact."

"Perhaps he was already in the room waiting for David to go into the mirror," Kong Ling said softly.

"No," David answered firmly. "I saw his face in the mirror and that only happens when you are coming out of the mirror."

"Maybe your mirror gets used to people going in and out," Robert said, moving his hands as if he were holding a mirror. "And your mirror stays somehow still sort of connected to the mirror world. Maybe this rogue, whoever he is, could find your mirror and was watching from the other side of the glass waiting for you to come through. Maybe he thought that once you were in the mirror the defensive systems would be shut down."

"Detective Nash," General Crossford said derisively, "I think you need to leave this to those who understand this phenomenon."

"No," David said loudly, "I think he's right... or sort of right. There must be a way to attach your mirror bubble to someone else's mirror, but only on the mirror world side. That's the only thing that makes sense. He'd never been in my mirror room, so he couldn't actually enter there, but he could look in and wait. I don't think it was so much that he timed it to when I went into the mirror as that when I stepped up to the mirror, he saw me and knew me. He had a name for me. He could come through, so he did."

"Maybe," Robert said, "it's like in that cartoon movie with the doors. Maybe there is a place of mirrors where you can look out through all the mirrors in the world and see all the mirror-walkers. It would just be a matter of finding the right window."

"I think you should have quit while you were ahead,

Mister Nash," the general said dryly.

"We can test Robert's idea," David said firmly. "I mean the first one," he added quickly. "I will go into the mirror trying to find The Intruder's mirror. If it works like Robert said, then I will have a window into wherever it is that he is based."

"Won't he be expecting you?" Momma Ling asked. There was obvious concern in her voice.

"Maybe," David said, "but I'm betting that he thinks that he is better and smarter than anyone else who has ever walked in the mirror." His voice dropped to almost a whisper as he said, "He might be."

He gave a weak smile to the general and added, "In any case, I'm pretty sure that he thinks we would never find out how he did this."

"Sometimes you gotta think outside the warehouse," Robert said with a smile.

"I'll explain that later," David quickly replied. "For now I need to test this idea. Give me a few minutes and we will know if this works."

"We will wait for you," the general said, motioning toward the door. David and Robert got up and walked through the torn up corridor toward his mirror room.

As they walked down the hallway Robert said softly, "You don't think this is going to work. You think you are going to end up facing The Intruder."

When David didn't say anything, he continued, "That's why you are doing this alone. You are protecting Chi."

David stopped at the entrance to his mirror room and turned around. "Yes, I'm not sure if this will work. Yes, I think I might end up facing The Intruder alone. Yes, I am protecting Chi... but not in the way that you think. I still believe The Intruder thinks she is dead. He pushed her through the barrier. He didn't see me actually fall through the barrier so he probably thinks I

136

pulled back out of the mirror before I fell through."

As he grabbed the doorknob, he sighed and said, "If I see him in the mirror, I will come back. I won't try to take him on alone." Then with a very firm voice he added, "But if I can see him *THROUGH* his mirror... then we've got him!"

Robert said nothing until David was standing in front of the mirror. Then he said quietly, "Let's be careful in there."

"Yes, Sergeant Esterhaus," David said sourly.

"Sorry," Robert said even more quietly, "I wasn't trying to be funny. And I wasn't trying to quote some old TV show. It just came out that way. I'm really worried about you."

David turned around. His face was totally blank and his voice was flat as he said, "If he catches me by surprise, tell Chi that I love her."

"She knows that," Robert responded. Then he said gruffly, "I served with some guys like you. You'd have made one hell of a Marine."

"I'd have never passed the physical," David said as he turned back to face the mirror.

A few moments later he was standing in front of what appeared to be a large window looking into what looked like a closet or perhaps a changing area in a doctor's office. It was small and shabby with a small bench against one wall. There was a worn curtain hanging at the entrance which could be pulled across the opening to give privacy.

His view of the room outside the closet was rather restricted, but he could see three men in old desert camo uniforms seated at a table. None of them had insignia or other identifying marks. There was evidently a fourth person at the table, but David could not see him at all.

The man facing David was speaking. "Viktor is not pleased," he said harshly. "You promised information and you didn't get it. And now you have spent the last few weeks chasing ghosts."

"They aren't ghosts!" the fourth person– probably The Intruder– said harshly. "They are dream-walkers like me. And if I don't track them down and take care of them, they will take care of me... and you... and Viktor!"

"Tell us who they are," the first person replied, "and we will take care of them. Viktor has operatives in every country."

"I don't know who they are!" The Intruder yelled. "If I did, I would tell you. The first one– the one who saw me– isn't really a dream-walker. I don't know how he saw me. But when I found him, two dream-walkers surprised me. One of them– a young Chinese girl– is dead. At least I think she is. I thought the other one was dead too, but he must have escaped me somehow. He's some kind of nerd. I think he's an American"

His voice softened as he said, "The facility I went to was definitely American, but there were Chinese soldiers there, too."

The first voice laughed, "Do you really think that the Americans and the Chinese are working together on some special, highly-secret operation that Viktor has not heard about?" He started slowly laughing again.

"What I know," The Intruder said harshly, "is that an American boy and a Chinese girl are after me. I know that whoever is backing them has a way to detect me. And I now know that they have weapons that can kill me while I am dream-walking. I thought the only way to kill a dream-walker was to throw them to the dogs, but now I'm not so sure. If they refine their technique I might not wake up from the next attack."

David found himself smiling as he listened to the anger and fear in The Intruder's voice.

"So what are you going to do now?" the first person asked as he stood up. "What do I report to Viktor when I go back downstairs?"

"Tell him to give me a week," The Intruder replied. "I have a way of watching them that they know nothing about. I'll set a trap and take care of this one. Then I'll find out if there are any more left on their side. If there are, I'll take care of them, too. After that, we are back to smooth sailing."

He got up and walked toward the mirror. David could see his face as he stepped into the small closet and pulled the cloth across the opening. "If you'll excuse me," he said, "I need to go see what my little nerd friend is up to."

Chapter Nineteen
A Leader Must Lead

David turned from the mirror yelling, "Out of the room. Out of the room, now!"

He and Robert literally ran into the hallway. David was yelling "Chi, Chi get out of your mirror room!" Robert threw him his robe and he quickly wrapped it around himself.

"She's not in the mirror room," Kong Ling said as she walked quickly up to him. "You said to let you act alone in this."

"Yeah," David said, looking past Kong Ling at Chi who was standing behind her. "And she's always listened to me," he added with a scoff.

Chi laughed and covered her mouth when Ling translated what David had said and then replied.

"She says," Ling said slowly, "that this time she knew you had to be alone."

"Conference room," David said firmly. "We have to talk. The Intruder is watching in my room, but for now he is wary of coming through the mirror."

"Getting shredded the last two times he came through might have something to do with that," Robert said with a big smile.

"Conference room," David repeated firmly and the four of them walked down the hallway toward their customary meeting room.

When they arrived, General Crossford was waiting in the room. So was the technical sergeant technician that had taken Lieutenant Anderson's place and his assistant. Chi's Chinese guards and David's Marine guards filed in behind them and took their stations along the wall.

"What's up?" the general asked as David, Robert,

Chi, and Momma Ling took their seats at the table.

"The mirror windows are real," David said quickly.

He looked around the room and continued, "The bad news is that we have to assume that he is watching us through any mirror that we have used. The good news is that I can watch him through his mirror."

"What did you learn?" General Crossford asked, pausing and looking at David hopefully.

"I don't know his real name or where he goes into the mirror," David answered. "He and three others were talking. It was a dingy room that could have been anywhere in the world. I couldn't see anything on the walls with writing on it. They never called each other by name, but they kept talking about someone named 'Viktor.'" He paused and pressed his lips firmly together as if thinking and then said, "But they never used a last name."

"So this Viktor is the boss," the general said. "We need to get that information to Lufton."

She nodded to the technicians sitting at the table.

"No!" David yelled as one of them started to rise to leave the room.

Everyone at the table startled and looked at him in surprise. "Don't transmit that information to anyone through official... or unofficial channels. They talked like this Viktor had a spy or spies that report back to him, even from within the US government. We don't know who that might be. The normal communication channels may be penetrated."

He again looked around the table and continued wryly, "As always, we don't know who we can trust."

"Then how do we communicate with Frank Lufton?" the general asked almost angrily.

"I have a special channel that is totally trustworthy," David answered.

"If you mean Marcus," Robert said, "how can you

141

contact him without going through the mirror? This rogue is probably waiting for you on the other side of the mirror."

"No probably about it," David said. "He is waiting for me like a hawk circling a field waiting for a mouse to come out into the open."

"Then what does this particular mouse plan to do?" Kong Ling asked. Like always, her voice hid any emotion that she might be feeling.

"The Intruder is going to be hanging around my mirror," David said calmly, "so I won't use it."

He took a deep breath and continued. "Instead, I will use a small mirror... something like a shaving mirror. What I'm hoping is that it won't be as connected to me on the first use."

He took a deep breath, then said, "Using a small mirror is a lot harder, but I've done it before– under worse circumstance." He smiled wryly as he remembered staring up the vent pipe in the bunker at the mirror which Momma Ling and Chi has lowered down in it. Then he shook his head to clear those memories of past battles. "I will use this small mirror one time," he said firmly. "Then it gets shattered... crushed... totally destroyed."

"There is a copper crucible up in the museum," the technician said. "They give demonstrations with it during the tourist season. We could bring it down here and melt the broken pieces."

"When the glass cools," David said, "give it to one of the pilots and have them drop it into Lake Michigan."

"You don't take any chances," the tech replied.

"I don't know how the mirror works– nobody does." David replied quickly. "We have to make absolutely sure with everything. The stakes are too high."

"So," Roberts asked slowly, "you think this will

work?"

"We'll find out when I go through the mirror," David said.

"When will that be?" the general asked.

"As soon as I leave here," David answered.

Turning to the technician, General Crossford asked, "Can you have the crucible ready when he gets back?"

The technician nodded his head and David stood up and turned to Robert, "Let's go to the small break room just inside the security perimeter," he said as he started for the door.

Robert didn't answer, but followed David out of the room. The two Marine guards trailed along behind them.

When they got to the room, David pulled a small mirror from his pocket.

"You already had this planned, didn't you?" asked Robert. It was more of a statement than a question.

"Yes," David answered. "I just hope I can find a supply of these small mirrors."

Robert laughed. "Don't worry," he said, "if they can come up with a couple hundred of those detectors overnight, a couple dozen mirrors should be no problem."

"Well," David said, "hopefully they can get some double-sided tape to go with them. I'm going to have to prop this up on the table and hope for the best."

"I could go look for something to stick it with." Robert said.

"No," David replied, "this will do. Besides, I've already texted Marcus to meet me."

"What if the general didn't agree to your plan?" Robert asked.

"As she, herself, said," David answered, "I am the leader of the mirror-walkers– whether I like it or not– and I'm the one who has to say how we can do this."

"Don't let it go to your head," Robert kidded. Then

143

is a false whisper he said, "Remember, Caesar, thou art mortal."

David just frowned at him and said, "Be quiet. This is going to be hard enough without your comments distracting me."

He then leaned forward and stared into the small mirror. After a few minutes, the soft sigh told Robert that David had successfully entered the mirror.

***

Marcus was waiting for him when he got to Chou's tomb. He stood silently watching as David walked closer to him.

"What do you need?" he asked.

"I have information for you," David replied. "Tell Frank Lufton that The Intruder works for someone named Viktor."

David hesitated and Marcus said, "There's more, isn't there?"

"Yes," David said, "and this is part of the 5% you *DON'T* tell Lufton anything about... at least not the specifics."

Marcus nodded.

"Evidently a mirror acquires a connection to the mirror-walker," David said. "If you know who the mirror-walker is, you can go to his or her mirror and look through it like it's a window."

"So he's watching you while you stand in front of the mirror?" Marcus asked.

"I'm not at my regular mirror," David said, "and the mirror I'm using is going to be destroyed as soon as I come out."

He then stood and silently stared at Marcus. After what felt like several minutes, Marcus said, "You want me to do something dangerous, don't you?" After a short pause, he continued in firm voice, "An officer doesn't know what it truly means to lead until he has knowingly sent someone to their death."

"That's not helping," David said angrily.

"It's a quote from one of my leadership classes," Marcus replied strongly. "It's harsh, but it's the truth."

He reached out and put a hand on David's shoulder to turn him so they were squarely face to face. then he continued, "I'm a soldier. I accept the risks. You are my leader. We are facing an enemy that only we can defeat. What do you need me to do?"

David remained silent for several moments, then said softly, "I need you to spy on The Intruder through his mirror. I really don't know what will happen if he comes through the mirror while you are standing there. He came through my mirror as I went in, but he intended to do that. I think he will just go right past you without knowing you are there, but... but... I really don't know."

"Can I go into his room once he has come into the mirror?" Marcus asked.

"Again," David said, shaking his head, "I really don't know. If he's standing there, you can enter using his face and calling him 'The Intruder,' but he would probably detect you, so that's out."

David stood thinking for a moment and then said, much calmer, "If you can figure out a name for someone else in the room, you should be able to enter. It doesn't have to be their true name, but it has to be absolutely unique or you have to be able to see him or imagine his image clearly in your mind. If you can't do that, something like 'the ugly one who guards The Intruder's mirror' might work."

He took a deep breath before continuing, "And I don't know if they have detectors like we do. If they detect you, then The Intruder will know there is another one of us and will start looking for you."

He paused again. "I'm pretty sure they don't have the same level of detectors we have or the rapid fire air Gatlings, so you are safe from that, at least."

"Gatlings?" Marcus asked in surprise.

"I'm sure Frank will show you them shortly," David said. "Just don't get on the wrong side of them."

"I'll report back when I've got something," Marcus said. "I'll use the plus ones code if there're any numbers." He then shimmered and disappeared.

Chapter Twenty
Waiting

David straightened up and looked around the room. Robert was standing beside him. "Do you want me to break the mirror?" he asked.

"Not yet," David said. "We need someplace where no slivers can be left behind."

"No sliver left behind," Robert said with a smile. "I will remember that."

A soft knock on the door interrupted them. "The crucible is hot and ready," a muffled voice said.

"Sounds like Sergeant McMasters found what we needed," said Robert. "Maybe we can just drop the mirror in the molten copper. Then there are no slivers to worry about."

"Let's go see," David replied, pulling his robe tight around his body.

When he opened the door, the sergeant and the two Marine guards snapped to attention. "No, no," David said in frustration, "I'm a civilian. No salutes. No attention."

Robert looked at them and said, "Just pretend he's the same as me."

All three soldiers smiled and tried to keep from laughing.

"That's better," David said. "Now let's get down to this crucible."

"Up, actually," said the sergeant. "That thing kicks out way too much heat to bring it into this wooden area."

"David," Robert said firmly, "I can't allow you to go outside the scanned and protected area."

"You're not my mother," David replied testily.

"No," Robert answered, "but they are." He was pointing at the two Marine guards. "And they have orders to keep you in the protected area."

"You can watch on the security cameras," the sergeant said quickly. "There are two set up out there to keep an eye on things."

"That'll have to do," David replied. "Where are the monitors?"

"The new security room is in housing area two, room four," the sergeant replied as he took the mirror from David's hand.

"Hopefully that will be a molten blob of glass at the bottom of Lake Michigan within the hour," David said as the sergeant hurried away.

***

Things did not go exactly as David had envisioned. While he, Robert, and several security people watched on the monitor, Sergeant McMasters turned the heat up on the device and slowly lowered the mirror into the glowing caldron using a set of long tongs. Evidently it was heated electrically because there were no propane tanks attached to it, only a very thick electrical cable.

One of the cameras had been moved so it pointed down directly into the steel bowl. There was already a molten pool of copper in the caldron. When the mirror first touched the golden liquid, it sputtered and spattered, but it was low enough in the bowl not to throw molten copper out into the room.

The mirror was gone within seconds. Sergeant McMasters let the caldron steam and smoke for a couple of minutes and then called out, "Ingot mold!"

One of the others brought what looked like a wooden shoebox over and set it on a ledge built into the frame next to the caldron. The sergeant carefully checked the position of the box and then pulled on a lever attached to the steel bowl. The bowl slowly tipped over, pouring the molten copper into the ingot mold.

After the copper stopped pouring from the caldron, the sergeant returned it to the upright position and dropped several chunks of orange material into the hot caldron.

He looked up at the camera and said, "Going to do a second batch of copper... just in case any glass or silvering is left in the caldron."

"Good idea," said Robert to the monitor.

"Thank you," replied the sergeant. Evidently there was a two-way audio feed to the area. "As soon as this cools a little," he continued, "we will put it aboard a bird and send it out over the lake."

"How long will that take?" David asked.

"About an hour," the sergeant replied. "The ingots will still be way too hot to handle, but they will be OK in the molds."

He pointed down at the steaming metal and said, "These are replica molds, so we can just chuck the whole thing out the door."

"Thank you," David replied.

The sergeant responded with a modified salute. He touched one finger to the side of his head and then pointed it at the camera.

"They know how important this is," Robert said, "and how important you are."

"Yeah, yeah," David answered, unsuccessfully trying to keep the anger out of his voice.

"It's the truth," Robert replied, sounding hurt.

"I know," David said, turning to Robert, "but I don't have to like it."

"What now?" Robert asked, brightening greatly.

"Now the mouse lays a trap for the hawk," David answered, "or at least, we confuse him a little bit."

***

On the way down the hallway, David explained his plan to Robert, and as soon as they opened the door to the mirror room, Robert began yelling at him, "I can't let you do this! You are far too important to this project. You are the last mirror-walker we have. We cannot risk you going into the mirror while that murderer is out there."

"I have to find him!" David answered angrily.

"And then what?!" Robert yelled back at him. "He'll just kill you like he did Chi. You're no match for him. Wait for the scientists and spooks to find him somewhere in the real world."

He stood staring at David. Their faces were only a few inches apart. "Don't make me call in the Marine guards," Robert said slowly. "We could always put you in a padded room with no reflective surfaces," he added ominously.

"OK!" David said feigning more anger. "I'll stay out of the mirror for the next four days, just like the general wants. But five days from now, I'm going into the mirror... with or without her consent."

"Good," Robert replied, putting his hand on David's shoulder. "Now come down to the conference room. The defenses are set to shred anything that's not flesh in this area. He's not coming in here for now." He then guided David out of the room.

Once the door was closed behind them, Robert turned and gave David a thumbs up. He started to say something, but David put his finger up to his lips and shook his head. He them mouthed, "Conference room," and walked down the hallway.

**

Once they were within the conference room, Robert

150

again asked, "Now what?"

"Now we wait," David answered. "We wait for Marcus and Frank Lufton to locate this Viktor and his minions."

After a long pause, Robert said, "It's harder waiting than doing, isn't it?"

"What?" David answered.

"Before," Robert continued, "you were always the one doing things and people like me had to sit around and wait. Now someone else is doing the doing and you are the one who has to wait to find out what is happening."

"Yeah," David said with a smile and laugh that looked and sounded hollow, "and it sucks."

"Welcome to my world," Robert replied.

"If we are going to sit and wait," David said, "and there's nothing else to do, we might as well watch TV and eat junk food."

"Now you're talking," Robert said, slapping his hand on the table.

A slight beep startled him. "I didn't do that," he said sheepishly, looking at the table.

"No, you didn't," David replied, holding up his phone. "It's a text... from Marcus."

"What's it say?" Robert asked.

David furrowed his brow and looked confused, "It says 'Hamlet 2.6'"

"That definitely doesn't make any sense," Robert said, shaking his head.

"I guess we have to look up what happens in Hamlet, act two, scene six," David said.

"Nothing," Robert said emphatically. "There is no scene six in act two of Hamlet. The second act only has two scenes. That message doesn't make any sense."

"How do you know that?" David asked. There was obvious surprise in his voice.

Robert looked slightly sheepish. "My minor in college was drama," he said. "Thought I might need the training for undercover work."

His face turned slightly red as he continued, "And yes, I still read Shakespeare... and other plays. I'm not a total Neanderthal."

"Never thought you were," David answered as he stood and started out the door.

"Where to now?" Robert asked.

"Security," David answered as they walked down the hallway. "We need to access the internet to see what Marcus might be trying to tell me."

"Is this some type of code you and Marcus agreed on?" Robert asked.

David blew out a short breath and answered, "We didn't agree on anything. He just said he would report if he found something important..." He stood thinking for a moment before adding, "... and then he said something about plus one for numbers."

"This is important," Robert said excitedly as he turned to face David, "did he say, 'plus one' or 'plus ones'? Or maybe plus one and one?"

"Uh..." David replied, "I think it was plus ones. ... Yes, I am pretty sure he said, 'plus ones.' Is that important?"

"Old downed airman code," Robert replied. "When you radioed for help, everyone, including the enemy would be listening to you. So you gave your map location coordinates with one added to or subtracted from each number... or with one added to the first and two to the second and so forth. Plus twos meant the same thing using the number two, and so on. The correct code was given to the fliers just before the mission. And to rescue forces on the ground like me."

"So?" David asked.

Robert looked up as if he were lost in thought and

152

then said slowly, "So... The Intruder is in Denmark."

"What!?" David exclaimed.

"Marcus said 'Hamlet 2.6' but what he meant you to read was 'Hamlet 1.4'."

David looked very confused and Robert continued. "Subtract one from the first number and two from the second and you get act one, scene four."

Robert was starting to talk faster, "The only really important thing that happens in act one, scene four–other than the ghost of Hamlet's father showing up," he said almost excitedly, "is when Marcellus tells Horatio that there is something rotten in the state of Denmark. Viktor is in Denmark."

"I need to talk to Marcus," David said.

"No," Robert answered firmly. "You need to wait. It's on Marcus' side of the table now. He has to make the next move. He will tell you when to come meet him."

"And if he doesn't?" David asked.

"Give him a day," Robert answered. "Then you can initiate contact."

He then gave David a big smile and said, "But for now, a big bowl of greasy, buttery popcorn and one of those comic hero action movies is calling my name down in the lounge."

"Shakespeare and comic heroes," David said with a laugh. "You do keep people guessing, don't you?"

"Ain't it the truth," Robert said as he pulled David toward the lounge area. "Ain't it the truth."

153

Chapter Twenty-One
Back Into the Small Mirror

David slept fitfully that night. Images from the super-hero movie they had watched in the lounge kept going through his head. Except, in his dream, the super villain had The Intruder's face and he was the super-hero. Unlike the movie, though, the super-hero was losing. Everything he tried failed. The villain slowly picked off each of David's friends until there was no one left except him... and Uncle Wei.

Dreams are strange things, so it somehow seemed natural to David that Chi's uncle would be fighting by his side. It was also obvious that Uncle Wei was a master of the martial arts— much more skilled than his niece— but The Intruder was even more skilled. It was a long and brutal battle, but finally the great scimitars were knocked from his hands. Surprisingly, he turned to David, smiled, and yelled out, "Victory!" just before The Intruder's blade cut him down.

That's when David woke up. His t-shirt and shorts were drenched in sweat. So were his sheets and probably his mattress. He looked around the room trying to fight down the panic that was overwhelming him. As he did, he startled and almost screamed aloud when he saw Detective Nash sitting in a chair in the corner watching him.

"Robert!" he yelled loudly. "What in the hell are you doing in here?!"

Robert looked back at him grimly and said, "I got tired of jumping up and checking on you every time you screamed." He huffed and said, "A couple of times, you were loud enough to bring the Marines over from across the hall." He stood up and stretched before continuing, "I thought about waking you, but you haven't gotten squat for sleep in the past week, so we decided to just let you dream, even if you were a bit noisy."

"I dreamed about The Intruder... and Marcus... and Chi... and Uncle Wei," David said flatly. His voice then turned slightly hoarse as he said, "Everybody got killed... except me."

"I hope I wasn't in your dream," Robert said, raising his eyebrows and shrugging his shoulders.

David startled for a moment and then said, "No, you weren't there. Just me and Chi and Marcus and The Intruder. Oh, ... and Uncle Wei."

"Sorry," Robert said. "This is hard on all of us, but especially on you."

"I need to talk to Marcus," David said firmly.

"No, you don't," Robert answered just as firmly. "You will wait until eighteen hundred hours this evening and then... if he hasn't contacted you, you can make contact with him."

He walked up and put his hand on David's shoulder. "You have to let him do his job," he said softly. "You are the leader now. Lead."

David looked at him angrily. Once or twice his jaw moved as if he were ready to say something, then finally he just sighed and said, "OK. Six o'clock." He then straightened up and said through clenched teeth, "But if I haven't heard from him by then, I go through the mirror looking for him."

"Now you're acting like a leader," Robert said with a smile, "checking up on your underlings."

"Yeah," David said flatly, "I'm becoming a leader." He paused and said, "If you don't mind, I need to shower and get dressed."

"I'll be next door," Robert said as he walked through the door connecting David's room to his.

***

David remained unusually tense throughout the day and Robert was uncharacteristically subdued and quiet. They spent most of the day in the lounge watching mind-numbing daytime television programs or cartoon hero movies. Chi and Momma Ling stopped by once or twice, but their quiet conversations were very short. It was obvious that Chi felt she should go back into the mirror to help David. At one point his voice rang out angrily as he almost shouted, "No! We have him convinced that you are dead. You have to wait on this side of the mirror until Frank Lufton tells us that it is clear."

A moment later, David's voice was much softer. He was asking Kong Ling to convey his apologies to Chi. "Tell her I can't wait until we can speak once again in the mirror, but it is just too dangerous right now."

Chi and her grandmother had just left the room when David's phone chimed, indicating a text. He looked at the screen and read, "Chou's tomb, 15?"

David immediately replied with a "K" and signaled Robert to follow him back to the small break room. When they got there, a large, lead box was waiting for them on the small table.

"Two dozen high-quality, silvered-glass shaving mirrors," the tech sergeant said as they came into the room. "And the crucible is heating up for the one you use."

"Why the lead box?" Robert asked.

"I don't know that we don't need it," he replied. "And as you said, we have to make absolutely sure with everything. The stakes are too high."

"I don't know that we don't need it, either," David said as he opened the box, "so it's a good idea. I like the way you think."

There was a small wooden easel waiting on the table. David set one of the small mirrors in place and began relaxing down. Soon a deep breath signaled that he had successfully entered the mirror.

***

Marcus was waiting for him at the tomb. "We found Viktor," he said as soon as David arrived. Then he added, "... or at least, we found his hideout."

"In Denmark?" David replied.

"Yes," answered Marcus.

"How did you know?" David asked.

"Frank is very sharp," he answered. "He asked me to look through the mirror at the electrical outlets and then draw them as accurately as I could when I got back. They looked like smiley faces. There were two horizontal flat slots for the eyes and something that looked like a mouth circle under them that had a flat spot on the top. Frank says that type of plug is used only in Denmark. He also said that he's tracked down people that way from photographs they were stupid enough to post on the internet, or in the old days, send to relatives."

"Then you went into The Intruder's base?" David asked.

"No," Marcus replied, looking almost ashamed. "I failed there," he said sullenly. "I tried to home in on one of his guards, but I must not have been concentrating hard enough because I almost ended up where the dogs are." He gave a hollow laugh and said, "I was right on the edge of what you call my mirror bubble and the darkness was starting to flow over me. Luckily I was able to pull back as soon as I saw the glow of the flames. I don't know what would have happened if I had fully gone in there."

"I do," David said. "You were very lucky."

"I try to make my own luck," Marcus replied.

"That's one of the reasons I didn't try centering in on the guards again. I just watched through the mirror. The Intruder stands and stares at his mirror a lot even when he's not walking in it. I sometimes thought he could see me, or sense that I was there. He came through once while I was on the other side of the mirror, but he went right past me to wherever he was going. Another time, it looked like he was staring right at me and I got out before he came though."

He grinned at David and said, "Like I said, I make my own luck."

"Regular luck also helps," David said. "Don't forget that."

"I just hope Viktor isn't as lucky as me," Marcus said.

"Are Viktor and The Intruder still at the same place?" David asked.

"We don't know," Marcus answered quickly. "Frank is pretty sure where this Viktor is. If he's right, then Viktor is in Malmo. We're hoping that's also where The Intruder is."

"How long before he's sure who Viktor is and finds him?" David murmured angrily.

"I think he already has," Marcus replied. "... found him, that is. He's still not sure who he is but he told me he would have a picture of him for me by tomorrow morning." Marcus suddenly looked very calm. "That's when I'm going through the mirror to do a recon around Viktor, himself. I'll have a name and a picture to tape on my mirror so I can concentrate on him."

"That should fit our timeline," David said. He was trying to keep the excitement out of his voice as he continued, "We have a trap set for The Intruder for four days from now. He thinks I am staying out of the mirror until then. Tell Mister Lufton we need to coordinate our attacks. If I can keep him distracted in the mirror then his flesh body is vulnerable." David grimaced and added, "Trust me, I know."

"Will do," Marcus replied. "I will talk to Frank tonight. I will signal you tomorrow at the same time, sixteen - thirty hours."

"I'll be waiting," David said as Marcus shimmered and disappeared.

Chapter Twenty-Two
The Face of Evil

David slept well– or at least better– but was no less agitated as he waited a second day for Marcus to report. Robert tried to cajole him into eating, but at breakfast and then again lunch he merely picked at this food. Chi joined them in the small lunch room, but David barely acknowledge her and remained mostly silent.

"You have to eat something," Robert said forcefully. "I've seen what going into the mirror does to you. You need to keep up your strength."

David stared at Robert silently for a long time before finally speaking. "My strength won't make any difference!" he said curtly. "The Intruder is better trained and more skilled that I am. At best, I can delay him for a short time while Frank's men attack Viktor's place."

He paused and then said very flatly, "I think we both know how this is going to turn out."

Robert said nothing. But Chi– when Momma Ling translated David's words– cried out and left the room sobbing. Kong Ling hurried out behind her.

"Chi knows how it has to end, too," David said.

Robert opened his mouth, but before he could say anything, David's phone beeped. Marcus was checking in a little early.

David looked down at the message and then held up his phone. It read "Tomb 9-1-1."

"Something's wrong," David said tersely. "I need to go talk to Marcus." He then walked hurriedly down the hallway toward the small break room and the lead chest of small mirrors.

When they entered the room, the tech sergeant was on the intercom telling his men to turn up the controls on the crucible. "Didn't expect you until this evening," he said. "The Marine guards tipped me off that you were on your way."

They were distracted by a loud noise from the security monitor. A tech was clanging the heavy iron dipper against the thick kettle-like crucible. He looked up at the camera and said, "I turned everything to max. This should be hot enough to melt your mirror by the time you get back."

"Thank you," David said to the monitor as he pulled a mirror from the lead chest and set it in the holder on the table. He had to force it slightly, but he soon felt the tug of the mirror and was with Marcus at Chou's tomb.

"Frank needs to talk to you," Marcus said tersely as soon as David arrived.

"How soon?" David asked.

"Now," replied Marcus. Then he said, "Maybe I should have said he needs to talk 'at' you. I'll go back with your answer."

David looked at Marcus, took a deep breath, and then asked, "Do you know how to transfer from place to place without coming out of the mirror?"

Marcus shook his head and David said, "Just concentrate on Frank Lufton's face and say or think his name real loud." He smiled at the captain and said, "It's just like when you go into the mirror, only harder. You've got to really concentrate."

Marcus nodded at him and then took several deep breaths as he slowly said aloud, "Frank Lufton, Frank Lufton, Frank Lufton."

David waited until Marcus was shimmering before saying firmly, "Frank," and moving to Frank Lufton's office. He was surprised that there was now a rather large mirror mounted on the wall directly in front of Frank's desk. He smiled when he realized that there was also a set of heavy, flat black, metal shutters which could be used to completely seal the mirror.

Frank was busy working on something, but there was a timer counting down on his computer. When it chimed, Frank looked up and said, "I am assuming that you, David, and hopefully, you, Marcus are here." He chuckled and said, "It'd better be you." Pointing at the ceiling, he continued, "My detectors say that there are two mirror-walkers here in the office with me."

His voice then got very serious. "We've identified Viktor," he said slowly. "Denmark is a small country if someone is looking really hard for you."

He blew out a long breath, almost as if he were smoking a cigarette. His face became blank, but somehow conveyed great anger. "I wasn't sure until we got the pictures this morning," he said flatly. "I thought he was dead," he continued harshly. "Everyone thought he was dead."

He paused for a long time and then continued. "His name is Viktor Popov. He's the type that gives mercenaries a bad name. He was indicted and tried in absentia for three separate counts of war crimes by the International Criminal Court at The Hague. They issued warrants for his arrest. I even had a contract to bring him in, but he died in a plane crash before anyone could close in on him. ...or so everyone thought until today."

He began drumming on his desk with his fingertips. It was obvious that he didn't want to say what came next. Finally he put both of his hands flat on the desk and said quietly, but firmly, "This man is ruthless... very ruthless... and I don't mean ruthless compared to the rest of humanity. I mean ruthless compared to me... and men far worse than me!"

He moved his hands nervously on the desk and looked from side to side as if checking that he was alone before continuing. "This could get very wet. Extreme measures may be needed to prevent significant collateral damage. I can't guarantee that I can bring in your rogue mirror-walker alive. In fact, keeping him alive may put a lot of innocent people at risk. Viktor killed 178 innocent people on that airliner just to fake his own death. Who knows what he might do to escape again."

He shrugged and then said in a measured voice. "I know I've got a blank check, but not everyone agrees what that exactly means. I need to know absolutely if I am authorized to kill the rogue if I have to. And..." He paused a long time before saying with deep breath, "... if moderate collateral damage is acceptable."

He looked down at a large scale map on his desk before saying, "Viktor has located himself in the middle of a densely-populated area. He knows that limits what most legal forces can do against him. He may have the whole building– or even the whole block– booby-trapped to ensure maximum collateral damage and chaos so he can escape during an attack."

He pressed his lips together for a moment and then said tersely, "It's what I would do in his situation."

Frank looked up at the area of the office where his detectors told him that two mirror-walkers might be standing. "If we meet heavy resistance," he said in a measured tone, "I will have no choice but to saturate the entire house with needle Gatlings mounted in tactical vans. My armaments experts say that will break up any improvised bombs– perhaps even without detonating them. We will have to make sure the house directly behind him and perhaps those alongside him have been emptied, but there still may be civilian casualties."

He tapped his hands on the desk. "Obviously," he said, "the chance of anyone in the house withstanding that fusillade is very small. If that's the way it plays out, there will be no survivors."

He stopped tapping and once again put his hands

together on the desk in front of him. "When it is all over," he said in a more normal voice, "I and my men will identify everyone who had been in the building. I will arrange for the rogue mirror-walker's body to be sent back to DC." His entire body stiffened and he spoke through clenched teeth, "... but I will personally deliver Viktor's body to The Hague as final proof that he is verified dead."

David listened carefully and then turned to Marcus. He spoke slowly and carefully. "We'd rather have The Intruder alive," he began, "and we would prefer no civilian casualties, but tell Frank that the decision is his."

The reality that he had just possibly condemned innocent people to death overwhelmed him and he stood silently staring at Marcus. Finally he said sadly, "That makes it up to you to come up with an alternative plan that doesn't involve blowing up a whole city block or shredding a townhouse full of people in a crowded foreign city."

"Thanks a lot," Marcus said as he shimmered away. Moments later he walked into the office to join Frank and David.

Frank looked up at where David was standing and said firmly, "Mister Malone, I want you to know that this is personal for me. You know that I am a man of my word. We were in... it doesn't make any difference where it was. Both Viktor and I were working for a tin pot dictator trying to subdue a rebellion. The rebel village agreed to surrender to me in return for a promise of safety. There were no combatants in the village. It was just old men, women, and small children."

He paused as if watching something that no one else could see, then he continued. "I promised them safe passage to the border," he said flatly. Then his voice became slow and filled with anger. "But Viktor and his men," he said, "machine-gunned them as they walked down the road."

He looked up again to where David was standing. "I switched sides," he said with a slight smile, "and brought down that pompous buffoon of a dictator in less than a week." His eyes widened slightly. "I was already hunting for Viktor before the tribunal at The Hague labeled him a war criminal. He will not get away from me again."

The look on Frank's face was now truly frightening. David was glad he was not physically in the same room with him.

Frank continued, "When I went after Viktor, most of his men deserted him. He tried to disappear into the criminal underworld of eastern Europe, but I can be pretty persuasive. He slipped away from us at the last minute by using a false name at the airport. You could do that in those days. I was only minutes behind him at the airport and had people waiting for his flight to arrive. I really would have turned him over to the officials at The Hague, but he never arrived. The plane exploded in mid-air.

"There were rumors that I had caused the explosion just to take out Viktor," Frank said. Anger was again creeping into his voice as he added, "There was no way I could prove that I hadn't. And I couldn't honestly say that I hadn't considered it. I almost ended up in The Hague myself."

His voice became very loud and emphatic as he finished. "The only way," he said slowly, "that I can prove my innocence of that atrocity and to bring justice to those people machine-gunned on the road is to bring Viktor Popov– or his body– to the tribunal. He will *NOT* escape from me again. And there will be *NO* collateral damage if I can possibly help it."

He smiled at David. It was a very cold smile. "I

165

hope you understand now why I must do this my way," he said slowly.

David looked at both of them and said softly, "return."

***

As soon as David took a deep breath and turned slightly away from the mirror, Robert called out loudly, "What's up? Why the nine-one-one?"

"Viktor is Viktor Popov," David replied wearily. "He is responsible for atrocities in at least three different wars and was condemned as a war criminal by The International Criminal Court at The Hague in the Netherlands."

"And?" Robert asked nervously.

"He blew up a plane load of people to fake his own death about seven years ago," David continued. "Frank is afraid of what he will do if he thinks he is cornered. He wanted to know if he had to bring The Intruder back alive."

"What did you tell him?" Robert asked. From his tone of voice, he already knew the answer.

"I told him it was his decision," David said. He looked down and the floor and stifled a sob. "He thinks he might have to shred the entire house to keep Viktor from blowing up the neighborhood and killing a bunch of innocent people."

His voice became totally emotionless as he finished with, "A lot of innocent people might die anyway. This is personal for Frank and he is going after Viktor one way or another. But I told him it was his decision. In effect, I decided that innocent people might have to die in order to bring down The Intruder."

Robert looked at him for a moment and then said quietly, "Sometimes the only choices are bad ones, but

166

you still have to choose."

David looked up at him and said softly, "Do you know who you are quoting?"

Robert smiled and answered in a louder voice, "WHO indeed! Does it surprise you that I watch The Doctor?"

"You are a very interesting person, Detective Nash," David said, smiling slightly.

"Shhh," Robert replied, "don't tell anybody. It would ruin my image."

Chapter Twenty-Three
The Final Battle

The next three days passed very slowly. Twice, David went into the mirror to meet with Marcus. Now that Marcus had a picture, he was able to go into the mirror directly to where Viktor was. He discovered that he and his men– including the rogue– were staying in a three-story row house. Marcus was able to go up to the top of the stairs from Viktor's office and view the rogue's room, but he stayed out just in case. He was able to find out that there were always at least two men guarding the rogue, both when he was in the mirror and when he was not. Marcus was also able to go downstairs and observe that there were always four to six men guarding the entrances.

The most important thing that Marcus discovered, however, was that Viktor always ate a very light lunch and then went up to his office on the second floor to work at his desk. He demanded privacy for this and was alone there for two to three hours. All of his men, except those guarding the rogue mirror-walker, were ordered downstairs during that time. That created a window of opportunity for the attack.

"One o'clock Malmo time is seven o'clock here," David told Robert as they watched another comic book hero movie. Then he added firmly, "I go into the mirror at six-thirty tomorrow morning."

Robert shut off the TV and David continued, "As soon as Marcus signals us that The Intruder has gone into the mirror today, we fake another argument in front of my mirror. I say I'm going in. You tell me to wait until early in the morning because it's more likely he will not be in the mirror. That will also make him think that we don't know for sure where he is."

168

"What will you do then?" Robert asked. "Do you really think you can hold him off for a half-hour?"

"Not if I try to fight him," David said. "But if I just keep backing away from him... or try to talk to him... or something."

"In other words," Robert answered, "you have no idea what you are going to do."

"Again Detective Robert Nash is blunt and uncouth, but accurate," David answered.

"What if Chi were there to help you?" Robert asked.

"No!" David yelled angrily. "She stays out of the mirror until it is safe."

"Maybe Marcus could join you?" Robert added hopefully.

"He is untrained," David shot back. "He can barely move himself around in the mirror. The Intruder would put him through the barrier in an instant." He paused and then said, "Besides, he has to help coordinate the attack for Frank."

"So," Robert said slowly, "I guess you go through the mirror alone in the morning." He paused and said, "I really wish I could somehow help you."

"Thanks," David said, "but I'm afraid I have to do this alone."

His phone chirped. It was the expected text from Marcus.

David began walking toward the mirror room but then stopped and turned around. "There is one thing you can do," he said softly. "Make sure Chi stays out of the mirror." He looked like he was going to say something else, but stopped himself and resumed his walk toward the mirror room.

Robert let David enter the room and start to take off his robe before bursting through the door yelling, "No! You are not going into that mirror this afternoon. You

169

are going in first thing in the morning like we discussed."

"Give me one good reason," David yelled back at him.

"It's a direct order from the general," Robert yelled back. "She has some sort of intelligence that says he is less likely to be in the mirror at that time. That way, you can find him before he finds you."

"The general's been wrong before," David said warily.

"I've got a good feeling about this one," Robert said. "If you can't trust the general, trust my gut. Wait until morning."

"OK," David answered dejectedly. "I'll wait. But at oh-six-thirty, I'm going into the mirror looking for him."

"Good decision," Robert said, holding up David's robe so he could cover himself. "Now let's go back to the bedroom so you can get dressed and go get us some chow. I hear they're having pizza tonight."

Pizza was actually on the menu for the evening meal, so David's response of "That sounds good," needed no acting to make it believable.

***

David didn't have any nightmares that night, but it wasn't because he was more relaxed. It was because he didn't sleep at all. He could hear Robert snoring in the other room and was tempted to sneak down the hallway and visit Chi one last time. But that would mean waking Momma Ling, and he didn't want to do that. Instead he sat at his computer writing up everything he knew about mirror-walking. It was a little before six by the time he was satisfied with his final copy and took his computer down to the security room so he could email the file to both General Crossford and Kong Ling with instructions that it was to be read only in the event of his death. He then returned and knocked softly on the slightly-open door between his bedroom and Robert's.

"Showtime," he said firmly.

"Ready," Robert answered as he came into the room. As they walked down the hallway together, the two Marine guards fell in step behind them.

"Stay clear," Robert said loudly as he and David turned to enter the mirror room. The two guards stepped back into a doorway, one glancing nervously down at the needle Gatlings mounted at the end of the hallway.

"Make sure you stay away from here," Robert warned David. "Anything that pops in here gets shredded. Remember that."

"Not something I'm likely to forget," David said softly as he lay his robe on the chair next to the mirror.

He looked over at Robert, took a very deep breath, and turned to face the mirror. In a few moments his breathing became shallow and regular as he went into the mirror saying softly, "The Intruder, The Intruder."

"I've been waiting for you," a rough voice said.

"I know," David answered. He was surprised at how calm his voice sounded.

He looked around. They were standing in a grayness next to what looked like a slightly-frosted window. Glancing through the window, David could see himself standing with his arms out from his side. A little ways behind him, Robert was sitting in a chair which he had leaned back against the wall.

"Where are we?" David asked.

"Don't you know?" The Intruder answered with a sarcastic laugh. "It's the gray space between the real world and the dream world."

He made a motion with his hands and the bubble expanded. It was like standing on a city street in a dense fog. In the distance, there were several more windows shining dully through the dimness. Dim patches of light in the fog indicated more windows even further away.

"You know there's only one way to kill me," David said.

"Of course," The Intruder answered. He was starting to move in a circle to get between David and the windows. David circled with him so that they remained face to face.

"Throwing you out through one of these mirrors won't do anything," he said with a low laugh. "You're going through the other side into the darkness."

His laugh became louder, "No one ever returns from the place of darkness."

"I did," David answered.

"You only thought you did," The Intruder said with a smile. "I must have been in too much of a hurry and hit you hard enough to knock you out. My mistake, but you didn't go into the darkness. You passed out and came out of the mirror, just like when I get hit by those damn special machine guns you have deployed wherever it is you are based."

David glanced behind him. The glow of the mirror windows was now gone. Instead the fog was getting darker and was tinged by a flickering glow. They were approaching the barrier of the mirror bubble, or perhaps the barrier was approaching them.

"I know you won't believe me," David said quietly, "but this is a trap for you, not me. If you surrender to me, I promise you that you will not be harmed."

The Intruder began laughing loudly. He seemed to be barely able to control himself. "You!" he almost screamed, laughing and pointing. "You, a scrawny American nerd, are threatening me?!"

He stood with his hands on his hips in front of David and said firmly, "I promise you this, I will make it quick... at least on this side of the barrier. I can't promise anything on the other side."

David looked at him and continued in a calm voice, "I tried. But you give me no choice."

He glanced down at his wrist as if to read his watch and see if he had stalled long enough, but then looked back up quickly. He shouldn't have taken his eyes off The Intruder. He didn't even see the foot coming at the side of his head. He only felt the stunning blow, and then felt himself falling.

The Intruder caught him. "The trick," he said calmly, "is to hit just hard enough to stun, but not hard enough to knock someone out. That way you stay in the dream world until it is too late."

He laughed. In David's semi-conscious state, the laugh seemed to rumble like thunder.

"You will be my seventh," The Intruder said, smiling at David. "That makes you my lucky charm."

David could feel himself being lifted up into the air. The Intruder was holding him up above his head and moving closer to the barrier. David tried to think "Place of Fire," but his mind wouldn't focus. The Intruder moved his arms back slightly getting ready to throw David over the barrier into the Place of Chaos and Fire.

"So this is how I die," David thought as a strange calmness began to flow over him.

That calmness was suddenly broken as he– and The Intruder– dropped to the ground. The Intruder sprang back up yelling and cursing loudly. There was another voice matching his screaming. It was Chi!

"So I didn't get you either," The Intruder yelled angrily as he jumped to his feet. "That just means I have to finish with number six before I can get to number seven," he said with a tight smile.

"No!" David yelled. "Chi, go back! You can't defeat him."

"Then I will die saving you," Chi yelled back as she

173

once again dove at The Intruder.

Her attack was futile. The Intruder's move was almost too fast to see. Chi collapsed in midair and crumpled to the ground.

"See," he said, looking over at David and giving an evil grin, "just hard enough to stun, but not hard enough to knock out."

The Intruder then picked up Chi and held her above his head.

"I will just bring her back like I did before," David said calmly. "That's a trick you haven't mastered." He smiled and said, "I have. That means you have to kill me before you can kill her."

The Intruder looked confused for a moment, but then turned, still holding Chi above his head. "Then I guess I just have to make sure that you go through the barrier first," he said as he dropped Chi to the ground.

David wasn't sure if the drop had knocked Chi totally unconscious or it had caused her to recover enough to return to her mirror room, but as soon as she hit the ground, she shimmered and disappeared.

"Just you and me now," The Intruder said ominously as he raced toward David.

David seemed to still be stunned. He wasn't moving at all. But that was a ruse. He waited until just before the rogue reached him and dropped flat on his face.

With loud cursing, The Intruder pulled to the side and tumbled to the ground to keep from going through the barrier. "Nice try," he said as he jumped back to his feet. "But next time I'll come in a little slower."

David had moved along the edge of the bubble, but he was still standing at the edge of the barrier. "One last warning," he said as The Intruder moved slowly toward him, bouncing on the balls of his feet like a wrestler ready to take down an opponent. The kick was very swift, but David had anticipated it this time. He spun in place so that it almost missed.

He was now facing the barrier. He stood slowly shaking his head, making it look like he had been dazed by the kick, which was almost true. He was right at the edge of the barrier and could see the flames in the distant pit. Several of the dogs were right at the barrier looking in at him and The Intruder. But David wasn't looking at them. He was forcing his eyes out of focus and slowly repeating to himself, "See with all your body. See with all your body. See with all your body."

The colors were off and things seemed strangely distorted, but suddenly David was somehow looking behind himself directly at The Intruder's face. The rogue mirror-walker was moving slowly up behind him weaving slightly back and forth in case David turned to attack.

As The Intruder got closer, David was concentrating as hard as he could on the rogue's eyes. He knew that the eyes would tell him when to move. If he acted too soon, The Intruder would escape. If he was too late, he, himself, would be doomed.

There was a quick shift in The Intruder's eyes and David thought loudly, *"Place of Fire."*

The Intruder hit him hard at waist level, but David was already shimmering in transfer and there was no substance to his body. The Intruder tumbled through David's shimmering body and rolled through the barrier into the darkness. When the rogue jumped to his feet, David was standing before him enveloped in a thin bubble that conformed to the shape of his body.

"I warned you," David said, "but you wouldn't listen."

The Intruder looked around assessing the situation. He knew that there was no escape from the Place of Darkness, but he was not the type to give up easily.

"You still have one chance," David said firmly. "If

you can defeat one of the Fire Warriors, you can take his place. Otherwise, you are food for the dogs or meat for the fire."

One of the Fire Warriors was approaching them. He was slowly swinging both of the huge scimitars in circles with his hands. "Do you dare to challenge me?" the warrior asked haughtily.

"Damned straight!" The Intruder answered loudly.

The warrior slid one of his scimitars across the ground to The Intruder. "Pick it up, if you dare," the warrior said loudly, "but if you do, your death will be slow and painful."

The Intruder grabbed the large sword and held it in front of himself with both hands. As he did, armor appeared on his body. Soon he was dressed almost identically to the Fire Warrior except his armor was glossy black while the Fire Warrior's was now bright red.

"What are the rules?" The Intruder asked curtly. "How do I win?"

"No rules," the Fire Warrior answered, just as curtly. "Whoever does not die, wins."

The Intruder immediately lunged forward in a vicious attack, swinging the heavy sword with ease. It was obvious that he had trained on a similar heavy weapon and knew how to use it.

The Fire Warrior deflected the attack and stepped slightly to the side so that the distant fire could be seen roaring between them as David watched the savage battle. This was not the thrust and parry of fencing or sabers. These were heavy weapons which swung with the weight and inertia of a battle axe. The noise of the battle was almost overwhelming. Sparks flashed as again and again one or the other would swing a death blow only to have it deflected at the last moment.

Both men were now moving in almost a ballet of

death as they swung in attack and then changed the blade slightly to fend off their opponent's counter attack. Both scimitars were swinging in wide circles as the fighters kept their swords in motion so that their opponent would not have a clear path of attack. The two circles seemed to be getting wider and wider until the tips of the swords were just barely missing the ground as the heavy blades swooshed past.

The dogs– or whatever they were– had now gathered in a circle around the fighters. They were staying well back out of range of the swirling blades, but were tensed and ready to rush to the feast of whomever finally fell.

David wasn't sure what finally happened. Perhaps the Fire Warrior was getting tired. Perhaps his sword dragged on the ground. Perhaps it was all part of The Intruder's plan of attack from the very beginning. In any case, it was over in a second. The Intruder, with tremendous effort and a loud grunting roar, suddenly stopped the spinning of his blade in mid-circle and plunged it directly at the chest of the Fire Warrior.

The huge, curved, scimitars were not made for stabbing. They were for slashing and hacking, so perhaps the Fire Warrior did not expect such an attack. In addition, a stabbing attack exposed The Intruder's arms while he did it. If the Fire Warrior had been expecting such an attack it would have been disastrous, if not fatal, for The Intruder. But for some reason, the Fire Warrior did not strike as The Intruder lunged, and the curved blade plunged through his armor and deep into his chest.

David watched as the Fire Warrior's scimitar dropped to the ground. The armor disappeared, leaving the Fire Warrior naked with the huge blade still buried in his chest.

Uncle Wei turned to David. There was pain and

177

anguish on his face, but he forced a smile and yelled out, "Victory!"

David knew what he had to do. He rushed to Uncle Wei's side. Wei had warned David that if he touched him, he would lose his bubble of protection. But that was when Wei was a Fire Warrior. Once he was defeated and food for the dogs, it might be safe to touch him.

The Intruder laughed and pulled his scimitar back out of Wei's body. "Looks like I don't die after all," he boasted proudly.

"No," David said angrily, as he cradled Uncle Wei in his arms, "you don't die."

He held Wei tightly and said bitterly, "You stay here forever." Then he shouted, "Welcome to Hell!" as both he and Uncle Wei shimmered and disappeared.

Chapter Twenty-Four
Report from Malmo

David turned from the mirror screaming, "Chi! Chi! Mirror! Now! Your place in Penglai!

He ran naked from his mirror room to Chi's. When he burst through the door, Momma Ling was holding Chi tightly while Chi was screaming and yelling, trying to get back in front of her mirror.

"She has to go back into the mirror," David said. "She has to go home to Penglai... NOW!"

"She heard you," Kong Ling said in her always calm voice. "And she understood you," she added as she released her granddaughter so she could stand in front of her mirror.

David didn't bother to explain further, but ran back to his mirror and took several deep breaths to calm himself. Finally his heart slowed and his breathing evened and he said strongly, "Chi's bedroom."

Chi was waiting for him in front of her ancient bronze mirror when he appeared in the room. "We must go to Uncle Wei," he said firmly.

Chi looked at him in confusion, but he beckoned her and they walked through the house to a small room built to be slightly apart from the main house. Chi gasped when she saw her uncle lying on the small cot. He had not aged in her lifetime, but was now showing gray hair and wrinkled skin.

He looked over at her from his bed and smiled. "I can see you my little Chi," he said in a shaking voice. "Your Beloved saved me and brought me back." His eyes closed and Chi ran forward to put her hand on his and to stroke his now very-wrinkled brow.

Looking up at David, Wei said, "There is no way I can repay you for bringing me back so that I can join my

179

ancestors. My father is proud of you and the way that you have become a Master of the Mirror."

He smiled once again at Chi and said, "Goodbye, my little Chi." He then gave a deep sigh and lay still. What lay on the bed now looked like the body of a very old man.

"He was only my Mother's age," Chi said, stroking his hand. "He looks so much older than he should."

"There is so much about the mirror that we cannot understand," David replied. "I had no idea what would happen when I brought him back."

"You brought him back?" Chi asked softly. Her face, but not her voice, betrayed her surprise.

"The Intruder took his place," David answered. He realized the harshness of his tone and continued in a much softer voice, "I tricked him into going through the barrier."

Chi's eyes widened in fear, but she said nothing.

"I let him push me through the barrier," he said slowly, "but I went to the Place of Fire just as he hit me." He gave her a weak smile and added, "He lost his balance and fell through the barrier."

"So he is dead," she said flatly.

"Not dead," David replied. "He is a Fire Warrior now. ... And I wouldn't expect any acts of mercy from him should we ever go there again."

"We must return and tell Momma Ling what has happened," Chi said.

David nodded silently and they both shimmered and left.

***

When David turned from the mirror, Robert was standing there holding his robe. "I know," David said with a smile, "you can tell when I'm coming out of the mirror."

"That," Robert answered, "and I think you've done enough streaking around here for the day."

"Oh, yeah," David replied. "It was kind of important that Chi join me in the mirror."

"Did you need her help with the rogue?" Robert asked.

"No," David answered, "I wanted her to see her uncle before he died."

"Uncle Wei?" Robert said in surprise. "I thought he was one of the Fire Warriors."

"He was," David said, "but I arranged for someone to take his place."

Robert smiled and said, "This gets curiouser and curiouser."

"You ought to see it from my side of the rabbit hole," David replied.

General Crossford's voice on the intercom cut them off with, "Mirror personnel and support staff to the conference room immediately."

"Ah," Robert said, "the boss wants to see us."

"Let's stop past my bedroom first," David said firmly. "I want to be dressed when I go to this meeting."

***

Robert and David were the last to arrive. He noted that the entire team was together again. Special Agent Mark Nash sat at the head of the table next to General Crossford. Lieutenant Harold T. Anderson was once again in the technical chair. The two tech sergeants who had filled in for him were standing by the wall alongside the Marine guards.

"I have a situation report from the team in Malmo," the general began. "The target was neutralized with only one casualty. Danish police and government officials raised a lot of hell about us operating inside Denmark without coordinating things with them, but when they saw that Viktor had wired explosives throughout the whole block of townhouses and even under the nearby streets, they softened their tone. They were also given jurisdiction on the eight mercenaries who surrendered."

"One casualty?" David asked

"Frank Lufton is one mean-assed, S.O.B." a voice from the wall monitor said.

David looked up at the wall and then said to those around the table, "In case you haven't met, this is Captain Marcus Robinson. Our liaison with Mister Lufton."

Various heads nodded and Marcus continued. "He pulled up in front of the row house with two vans and a big truck disguised as a power company vehicle. I went into the mirror from a van around the corner and confirmed that Viktor was sitting in his office, then went back to report to Frank who was waiting with the truck.

"As soon as I told him Viktor was in his office, he gave a signal and the boom on the big truck raised up. The boom had one of those bucket things on it, but it wasn't a bucket. It was a special box with four of the Gatlings mounted in it. It raised up to second story level. There was a thirty-second burst and a hole the size of a room appeared straight through the house and maybe the house behind it.

"After that, Frank walks up to the door calm as could be and rings the bell. Nobody answers, so he yells, 'Your boss is dead. You have to the count of five to surrender or die.'

He yells that again and the door opens real slowly. 'Surrender or die,' Frank says pointing across the street to where the two vans were sitting. Their sides were now open and you could see four more of the Gatlings pointed directly at the house. 'One last time,' Frank says to the guy standing in the doorway, 'surrender or die.'

"After a little pause, six guys walk out with their hands in the air. Frank stops the last one and tells him, 'Look at the big truck across the street and then tell your friends upstairs to come out with you.'

"The Gatlings on the big truck were now level with the third floor. The guy went back in and a few moments later came back out with two other guys. They were carrying what looked like the body of our rogue mirror-walker."

"Thank you for your report, Captain Robinson." the general said.

She then turned to the group around the table and said, "Frank Lufton will arrange for the rogue's body to be shipped back to the US."

"He's not dead," David said firmly. "It's hard to explain, but it's more like he is comatose. His mirror self is permanently trapped in the mirror... in the Place of Fire. His body is still alive, but... he isn't there."

"Then we will arrange for him to be brought back on a hospital plane," the general replied, "and kept in a very secure hospital."

She paused to look around the room. "Frank Lufton," she said softly, "took possession of Viktor's body. He is planning to turn it over to medical authorities at The Hague so that it can be positively identified as Viktor Popov."

She glanced up at the monitor screen and continued, "Captain Robinson, you will be accompanying the comatose body of our rogue mirror-walker back to DC."

She turned to David and said, "Once he is back in the states, the captain will be taking your place in the testing and improvement of detection and defense against mirror-walkers. You will be happy to know that your services will no longer be needed."

"That isn't exactly true," David said very slowly.

"Oh?" the general replied.

"Marcus is untrained and could make terrible errors in the mirror," he continued, "...fatal errors for him or for others."

He looked around the table, "I propose," he said, his voice growing louder and stronger, "that we create a training camp for mirror-walkers. At that camp, we can teach them the basics of the mirror. We can also help them school themselves in the philosophies which should guide a mirror-walker... of any nation.

"And," he continued, "we can teach them some physical skills so that they can defend themselves, if necessary, within the mirror."

"Do you propose to do all of this yourself?" the general asked.

"Chi, and Marcus, and I," he answered, "can be the original teachers. As more mirror-walkers are discovered, others can take over the task."

"So you do expect that there are more mirror-walkers," Agent Mark asked.

David looked directly at Robert and said firmly, "There is a place of grayness which forms the transition between this reality and the reality of the mirror bubbles... just like Robert said there would be."

He paused a moment to let what he said sink in, especially to Robert, then he continued, "In the grayness you can see all of the active mirror windows."

He looked around the table and then answered the unasked question, "Yes," he said firmly, "there are more mirror-walkers." His voice softened to almost a whisper as he added, "... perhaps more than the world is ready for."

Epilogue
Chi and David at Home

"How many in this group?" David asked as he ran his hand slowly across the glossy marble that sealed Chou's tomb.

"Five" Chi replied. "They should be here soon."

She paused and then said, "Marcus has been delayed slightly. He has to meet with a new mirror-walker from India."

"So we might have six?" David replied.

"Five for now," Chi answered. "Number six is probably not yet ready to accept what is happening to him. Marcus has to show him first that the mirror is not evil."

David laughed dryly. "But it can be," he said flatly. "That is why we start here with each new group."

"We could tell the story just as well at the training center," Chi said quietly.

"There is more to the story than words," David said, once again touching the marble stone. "They must see this part of the story as well."

He looked up as the first of the group appeared. "Welcome," he said warmly.

"Welcome to the tomb of my grandfather," Chi said as two more mirror-walkers appeared.

The remaining two appeared shortly after that and David again said "Welcome."

Chi smiled at them and once again said, "Welcome to the tomb of my grandfather."

David looked out at the group, slowly meeting each person's eyes and said, "This is Chou's tomb," he said slowly. "Chou was a master of the mirror. He was very skilled in the martial arts. And he was my mentor. But he has joined his ancestors and walks in the mirror no more."

He turned slightly so he could see the shiny marble which sealed the tomb. "The day will come," he continued, "when one of you will stand before his tomb... or my tomb... or perhaps even Chi's tomb... and welcome a new group of mirror-walkers to this period of training.

"No real training takes place here," he said as he turned to again face the group. "We start here to remind you... and me... that being able to walk in the mirror does not make you good... or evil... or powerful... or immortal. Mirror-walking is a natural talent no different than being able to create great art or great music or great technical inventions. It is a skill that you can use for good or for evil. How you use that skill is what will cause you to be remembered through the ages."

To the surprise of some of the new trainees, he then shimmered and disappeared.

Chi stepped forward. "Our training site, for now, is located in a desert area in the state of New Mexico in the United States of America. Only the International Oversight Commission and certain members of the American Bureau of Land Management know we use that site."

She stepped forward so that she was centered on the line of novice mirror-walkers, "You came here by concentrating on David's name and face. It is time for you to go to that area by again thinking of David's face and name. Once you have made the transfer, I will join you there."

Three of the trainees almost immediately shimmered and disappeared. The fourth quickly joined them. The fifth, a young woman with flame red hair, stood looking at Chi for a moment, and then said, "I'm afraid."

Chi stepped up to her and took both of her hands in

her own. "I will transfer with you," Chi said with a reassuring smile. A moment later, they were standing in what looked like an old school house that had been converted into a museum.

"This was once a prosperous silver mining town called Valley Lake," David was saying. "The buildings are now mostly just ruins, except this one. It is currently a museum but was once a school house and community hall. It has desks we can sit at and a large, open area that will be important when Marcus and Chi teach you martial arts and self-defense. There are also trails into the mountains on which we can walk as we talk about the responsibilities of being a mirror-walker."

Chi waited until David finished and then said, "If you need to speak privately with David or Marcus or me, text us with 'Chou' or 'Tomb' and a time. We will try to meet you."

"Our group is scheduled to get back together again tomorrow at ten a.m. New Mexico time. Marcus will be with us then. You can return here by thinking about this room and saying, 'School House.' Until then, make sure you get enough rest. Staying in the mirror for an extended period of time is physically draining."

He laughed slightly and added, "And it sometimes takes a while to get used to the time change."

Chi again spoke. "David will again leave before you," she said brightly, "so you can once again see how you look to another mirror-walker when you leave."

David shimmered and disappeared.

"Until tomorrow," Chi said, bowing slightly to the group.

After all five of the novice mirror-walkers shimmered and disappeared, Chi said softly, "David's house."

***

David was already sitting in the living room when Chi arrived. "I have it set to start in about five minutes," he said as she appeared.

"I saw you watching this with Robert at the mine," Chi answered, "but I couldn't understand what was going on." She gave him a weird smile as she shrugged and said, "And it wasn't just the language. The whole movie just didn't make sense. That's why I asked to see it with you in the mirror."

"It's a cartoonish super-hero movie," David said. "I like them because it's easy to see who the good guys are... and the good guys always win."

"But it isn't reality," Chi replied.

"No," David answered, "it's a cartoon. In our reality, you can't be sure who the good guys actually are."

"And the good guys don't always win," Chi finished.

"But this time," David said, "at least one really bad guy got put away forever."

"And my uncle got to come home," Chi said.

"Yes," David said, "Uncle Wei got to come home... to die."

The movie started at that point and Chi snuggled down into David's arms.

THE END